"I need a husband."

Rosie sniffed. "But husbands don't grow on trees."

"No," Steve agreed. "Not the last time I checked."

Suddenly, her words sank in.

She needed a husband.

Then she could face her family and friends without shame. He owed her. He owed the family. There was a way to help them all. But it was a huge risk. He could lose the best friend he'd ever had, the only family he'd ever known.

But Rosie was part of that family. Shouldn't he help her? Shouldn't he do the honorable thing, the gentlemanly thing?

He wasn't a member of the family, not by blood. More than once he had wished there was a way to change that. Now he could do something for Rosie that none of the rest of them could. He had a way to get her out of this jam.

"I could be a husband," he said finally.

Dear Reader,

Happy Valentine's Day! What better way to celebrate than with a Silhouette Romance novel? We're sweeter than chocolate—and less damaging to the hips! This month is filled with special treats just for you. LOVING THE BOSS, our six-book series about office romances that lead to happily ever after, continues with *The Night Before Baby* by Karen Rose Smith. In this sparkling story, an unforgettable one-night stand—during the company Christmas party!—leads to an unexpected pregnancy and a must-read marriage of convenience.

Teresa Southwick crafts an emotional BUNDLES OF JOY title, in which the forbidden man of her dreams becomes a pregnant woman's stand-in groom. Don't miss *A Vow, a Ring, a Baby Swing.* When a devil-may-care bachelor discovers he's a daddy, he offers the prim heroine a chance to hold a *Baby in Her Arms,* as Judy Christenberry's LUCKY CHARM SISTERS trilogy resumes.

Award-winning author Marie Ferrarella proves it's *Never Too Late for Love* as the bride's mother and the groom's widower father discover their children's wedding was just the beginning in this charming continuation of LIKE MOTHER, LIKE DAUGHTER. Beloved author Arlene James lends a traditional touch to Silhouette Romance's ongoing HE'S MY HERO promotion with *Mr. Right Next Door.* And FAMILY MATTERS spotlights new talent Elyssa Henry with her heartwarming debut, *A Family for the Sheriff.*

Treat yourself to each and every offering this month. And in future months, look for more of the stories you love...and the authors you cherish.

Enjoy!

Mary-Theresa Hussey

Mary-Theresa Hussey
Senior Editor, Silhouette Romance

Please address questions and book requests to:
Silhouette Reader Service
U.S.: 3010 Walden Ave., P.O. Box 1325, Buffalo, NY 14269
Canadian: P.O. Box 609, Fort Erie, Ont. L2A 5X3

A VOW, A RING,
A BABY SWING

Teresa Southwick

Silhouette

R O M A N C E™

Published by Silhouette Books

America's Publisher of Contemporary Romance

To Mike Boyle,
a fellow forgotten middle child.
You're a hero in my book, bro.

SILHOUETTE BOOKS

ISBN 0-373-19349-1

A VOW, A RING, A BABY SWING

Copyright © 1999 by Teresa Ann Southwick

This edition published by arrangement with Harlequin Books S.A.

® and TM are trademarks of Harlequin Books S.A., used under license.
Trademarks indicated with ® are registered in the United States Patent
and Trademark Office, the Canadian Trade Marks Office and in other
countries.

Printed in U.S.A.

Books by Teresa Southwick

Silhouette Romance

Wedding Rings and Baby Things #1209
The Bachelor's Baby #1233
A Vow, a Ring, a Baby Swing #1349

TERESA SOUTHWICK

is a native Californian with ties to each coast, since she was conceived in the East and born in the West. Living with her husband of twenty-five years and two handsome sons, she is surrounded by heroes. Reading has been her passion since she was a girl. She couldn't be more delighted that her dream of writing full-time has come true. Her favorite things include: holding a baby, the fragrance of jasmine, walks on the beach, the patter of rain on the roof, and, above all—happy endings.

Teresa also writes historical romance novels under the same name.

Dear Reader,

Since I was a little girl, my two favorite things in the world have been books and babies. Even now, I can't help but peek into each stroller I pass. The power of a child to command the attention of every adult in a room amazes me. More extraordinary is the magic of a baby's laugh. I challenge anyone to keep from smiling at that joyful sound.

I specifically remember being bitten by the writing bug in the fourth grade. That "Pike's Peak or Bust" assignment I thought was completed wouldn't let me alone until I added a few more pages. My teacher liked it. More incredible was how much I enjoyed (gasp!) homework.

Not a day goes by that I don't give thanks for the gift of reading and the satisfaction and pleasure of writing—especially when I can include a baby in my story. So it's an honor and privilege to have *A Vow, a Ring, a Baby Swing* included in Silhouette's BUNDLES OF JOY promotion this month.

This book was a lot like that fourth-grade writing assignment. Creating Rosie Marchetti was great fun—not to mention her four attractive brothers and hunky hero! Every day I couldn't wait to sit down at the computer and see what the meddling Marchettis would do next. Steve Schafer stole my heart as he was capturing Rosie's. The only sight more endearing than a baby is a strong man holding that baby. Steve does that—and more.

I hope you enjoy reading Rosie and Steve's story as much as I loved writing it.

Teresa Southwick

Chapter One

No man had a right to look so good in a pair of worn blue jeans and a brown leather jacket that had seen much better days.

And no woman about to get married should notice, Rosie Marchetti told herself. She should especially not notice through the chapel window as she waited for her bridegroom.

What was *he* doing here?

Steve Schafer.

Her heart gave a medium-size lurch before she could stop it. How did he always do that to her? When would she learn not to let him?

She watched him look around the parking lot, then her hands began to shake when he headed her way. She wouldn't have noticed him out there if he was just any man. But her luck wasn't that good.

Steve Schafer stood six-feet-two-inches, one-hundred-and-ninety-pounds of swaggering sex appeal. Not just any man had his shade of sandy-blond hair, or mocking eyes that color of dark blue, or a jaw so square and hard it could have been chiseled from stone.

There was something about Steve. A masculinity that reached out to women—even ones about to get married—daring them to flaunt their femininity and force him to take notice. Rosie was no exception. It was her cross to bear. For as long as she could remember she had been searching for the antidote to his particular strain of seductive charm.

Every single time he hadn't noticed her, she prayed for a cure that never came. She winced at the thought, angry at herself for still caring—even a little.

So what was her brother's best friend doing here, at her *secret* wedding?

Then she knew. She'd been half expecting something; if not act of God, or a natural disaster, at the very least some form of interference from the meddling Marchettis. She pressed a hand to her stomach as the bad feeling she'd been fighting while waiting for her overdue groom to show up got worse.

Just last night she'd phoned home in Los Angeles about her plan to marry Wayne. Her mother had asked her to postpone so that she and her father could give their only daughter a big church wedding. Rosie explained that she and Wayne were madly in love with each other and couldn't wait. She was pleased that only half of that statement was a lie. Florence Evelyn Marchetti could spot a whopper a mile away. Rosie figured she'd had a fifty-fifty chance that her mother would buy the story. When they'd hung up, she'd *thought* her mother had accepted her plan to marry. If she'd thought right, it could mean that Steve was here with bad news that had nothing to do with the wedding.

Clutching her bridal bouquet of white roses and baby's breath, she rushed toward the man now standing in the chapel vestibule staring at her.

"Oh, God, Steve. Is my mother all right? She didn't have another heart attack did she?"

He removed his aviator sunglasses, but that didn't help her to read his expression. "Your mom's fine, Ro."

"Thank God," she said, breathing a sigh of relief.

She would never have forgiven herself if her announcement had brought on a relapse. Florence Marchetti's heart attack three months earlier had traumatized the whole family. It was like seeing a crack in the Rock of Gibraltar and watching helplessly while the indestructible stone crumbled. The doctor had told them that she was extremely lucky, there was no damage to the heart muscle. She would recover nicely. It was a blessing in disguise, a wake-up call for a healthier life-style.

So if Steve wasn't here about her mother, he was here because of the wedding. She shot him a suspicious look. "Mother sent you to talk me out of getting married."

He didn't deny it. He just glanced around the chapel with its abundance of plastic, the primary decorating motif. Plastic flowers exploded from plastic vases beside flimsy white plastic chairs that looked as if they wouldn't hold the weight of a pixie. If his expression betrayed his feelings, she couldn't tell. But she knew what he was thinking. She wasn't crazy about the ambiance, either. But a girl had to do what a girl had to do.

"This isn't your style." His voice was hard as he echoed her thoughts. Worse, there was censure in his eyes.

How would he know what her style was? He'd never given her the time of day, not since she was a child. For Pete's sake. Why did his indifference still bother her? She pushed that thought aside. She should be mad about *why* he was here. And she was.

Her parents had a right to disapprove of her decision. They didn't have a right to interfere—or send a proxy to do it for them.

She knew they weren't keen on Wayne. The Marchettis had made no secret of the fact that they thought their only daughter could do better. But they found something wrong with every man she brought home. Wayne wasn't a doctor, a lawyer, or a teacher. In fact, she wasn't exactly sure how he supported himself. But she liked him. Besides, he had one qualification they didn't know about. If her luck wasn't completely down the tubes, they never would.

"I'm getting married. There's nothing you can say to change my mind," she finally said, annoyed when the words came out defensively instead of in the cool, dismissive tone she'd been shooting for.

"You're making a mistake." He took her arm. "I'll buy you a cup of coffee and we can discuss this."

"I'm not going anywhere." She stared at his long, strong fingers curved around her upper arm. When she zinged him a look, he dropped his hand. "Wayne will be here any minute. He had some things to do. One of those errands was a surprise for me. He's such a sweet, thoughtful man." She wasn't sure whether she was trying to convince Steve or herself.

"No comment."

She'd certainly bowled him over with Wayne's good P.R. "You'd better go, Steve. No one's supposed to know about the wedding, and I've no idea how I'm going to explain your presence." The truth was she just didn't want him there when she took her vows.

"If you leave with me, you won't have to explain anything to anyone."

Her stomach clenched and she was instantly and forcefully reminded of why she was there. "I couldn't do that."

His eyes hardened with anger. "Wayne's a creep, Rosie. You deserve better."

"You sound like my parents." Her fingers curled around her bouquet until her knuckles turned as white as the roses. "They don't know Wayne the way I do. And neither do you."

"You got that right." Sarcasm dripped from every word.

No matter that just a few minutes before she had been having thoughts about Steve that no bride about to marry another man should have. Rosie felt obligated to defend her fiancé. She'd had a lifetime of family disapproval and the buttinskis had better get used to the fact that she was calling the shots. She was a grown woman; she knew exactly what she was doing. Steve Schafer had no right to stick his nose in and spoil everything.

"Wayne is not a creep. He's a wonderful man. He's thoughtful and kind and generous. And smart. And very good-looking. I'm going to marry him and you can't talk me out of it," she finished desperately.

"I was afraid you'd be stubborn."

"What's that supposed to mean?" she asked. "What's going on?"

Even as she demanded to be told the truth, a bad feeling settled over her. Wayne was way overdue and getting later by the minute.

There was a weary, disgusted look in Steve's eyes. Deep creases carved his face beside his nose and mouth. Something told her she wasn't going to like what he had to say.

"Wayne's not coming." His voice was flat.

She couldn't have heard him right. "I—" She stopped and swallowed hard. Numb. That's what she was. She couldn't feel anything and there was a part of her desperately grateful for that. "I don't believe you. H-he said he would meet me here at noon. It's only a few minutes past—"

"It's later than that."

"He'll be here." Her hands started to shake. "He has to," she whispered.

"What?" he asked sharply.

"Nothing."

"You can wait if you want, I can't stop you. But I'm doing my best to spare you, Rosie. Trust me. He's not coming." There was pity in his expression. It was that more than anything that made her eyes burn with unshed tears at the same time she wanted to deck him. How dare he pity her?

She blinked away the moisture. "What has Wayne ever done to give you such a low opinion of him?"

"Let's get out of here. I'll take you back to the hotel and buy you some lunch. We can talk—"

"I'm not leaving here until my groom shows up."

"I just told you, that's not going to happen." He

glanced at the watch on his wide wrist and nodded with satisfaction.

"How do you know that?"

"Because he's a weasel."

"That's not true and it's not an answer." She shook her head as her eyes widened. "I can't believe you're doing this to me."

"I wish I didn't have to." He met her gaze until she looked away. "Believe it or not, I'm not enjoying myself. Let's get out of here, go someplace private so we can talk. We'll get something to eat, then I'll take you back to the hotel for your things."

That was twice in two minutes that he'd offered her food. Apparently he thought the world-famous Marchetti method of eating one's way out of a crisis would cure what ailed her. But he was so wrong.

She pointed an accusing finger at him. "You're trying to break us up. You want to hustle me out of here before Wayne arrives and make him think I stood him up."

"Your imagination is working overtime."

"That's what you'd like me to think. I'm just going to wait. And I don't need company. Feel free to leave anytime."

Behind her, the chapel door opened and a man, dressed in a dark suit and carrying a book in his hand, slipped inside. He walked down the carpeted aisle and stopped in front of them. "Finally. This is the tardy bridegroom?" he asked, staring questioningly at Steve's worn leather bomber jacket, white cotton shirt, and faded jeans.

Rosie shook her head. "He was just leaving, Your Honor. Wayne will be here any minute."

"Steve Schafer," Steve said, holding out his hand to the justice of the peace.

"Charles Forbes."

After they shook hands Steve said, "There's been a change of plans. Miss Marchetti won't be getting married today after all. We're sorry to have inconvenienced you, Your Honor."

"Not so fast, buster," Rosie said. "I'm not sure what he's trying to pull, Judge Forbes. But if you'll be patient for just a few more minutes, my fiancé will be here."

"He's very late." The judge gave her a look, puzzled, but definitely sympathetic, too. "We can wait until my next couple arrives. But I've a busy schedule this afternoon. I squeezed you in today, Miss Marchetti, remember?"

She winced at the "Miss." It should have been "Mrs." by now. "How could I forget? Just a little longer. Please. He'll be here. I'm sure of it."

Steve shook his head. "There's no point in wasting the man's time, Rosie. Wayne's not coming."

"How can you know that for sure?" she asked again. She was really afraid he would answer the question this time, and her desperation increased in direct proportion to her groom's tardiness.

Steve glanced at the judge, then down at her. "Let's go outside—"

"No. I'm not budging one step until you tell me, right here, right now, how you can be so sure Wayne's not coming."

Steve's mouth thinned and he looked down for several seconds. Then he met her gaze squarely. "I know because I gave him a lot of money and a plane ticket as far away from you as he could get without a passport. Then I drove him to the airport and waited until his plane took off. Wayne's not coming to marry you today or any other day, Rosie.''

Steve tipped the room service waiter and shut the door to Rosie's hotel suite. She'd been in the bathroom ever since he'd brought her here from the chapel. It had been almost an hour and if she didn't come out soon, he'd have to break the damn door down. One corner of his mouth lifted. You could take the kid out of the gutter, but apparently you couldn't completely leave the gutter mentality behind.

He knocked softly. ''Lunch is here, squirt.''

''I'm not hungry.''

''I ordered a bottle of wine.''

''It's not even close to happy hour,'' she said. The door between them did nothing to muffle her sarcasm.

He knew he should be grateful she wasn't in the same room with him. An angry Marchetti was a formidable sight. When her shock wore off, he would be in for it. Unless he could mellow her out with a glass of wine.

''It's the kind you like. I figured it was the least I could do.''

''You figured wrong. And how would you know what I like?''

He knew. For years he'd covertly watched Rosie at family gatherings and carefully filed away every detail he'd observed about her. Oh, yeah, he knew damn well.

After a few moments she said through the door, ''Just go away and leave me alone.''

Steve turned his back, trying to shake the feeling that he'd slam-dunked a kitten. He ran a hand through his short hair. He'd done the job he'd been sent here to do. He was the hatchet man, not Dear Abby. He didn't have to stay; the cabin was waiting. The Marchettis had offered him the use of the family vacation home in the mountains. He hadn't gotten away in years and, after today, he was looking forward to the isolation more than ever. There was a good chance of snow since it was the middle of January. Holidays were over. Tourists would be gone. He could hardly wait. But he couldn't walk out on Rosie just yet. Not until he got her the hell out of that bathroom and home to her mother.

He looked around the hotel suite, taking in the elegant understated decor. Matching cherrywood furniture polished to a perfect shine decorated the bedroom, parlor and dining area. The sofa, love seat, and accent chairs in shades of blue, green and mauve striped and floral patterns had been expertly coordinated by an interior designer. Expensive Stiffel brass lamps held court on all the tables. Who'd have guessed that a guy like him could even get into a place like this? The years had smoothed away the rough edges of the skinny, dirty kid he'd once been.

A kid who'd never laid eyes on his father. A kid whose mother had dumped him at a downtown L.A. bus station never to be heard from again. He'd wound up in the county home with other kids just like himself, angry and bitter. The odds said he should have gone to hell.

He heard a faucet running in the bathroom. Rosemarie Teresa Christina Marchetti. He smiled. He'd beat the odds when a twist of fate had crossed his path with her brother Nick's. They'd become best friends and the Marchettis had taken Steve under their wing.

He heard her moving around and his smile turned grim. He wasn't sure which was worse: her self-imposed quarantine, or facing her when she came out. He wasn't looking forward to the angry third-degree he knew she would give him. There was only one thing worse than that.

Seeing her cry.

She hadn't yet. As a matter of fact, she hadn't said much, either. That zombie-like calm was so unlike her it made him nervous. As much as he dreaded the inevitable storm, it would be preferable to the silent treatment. He hated waiting for the other shoe to fall—or in this case, the flood of tears he knew was coming. He had to get her the hell home—to someone who *could* hold her when she cried.

The door behind him opened. He braced himself.

"Steve?"

"What?" He turned.

Her hands twisted together as she stared accusingly at him. She had changed out of her beige silk suit and looked just as pretty, maybe more so, in a denim jumper with a white T-shirt underneath. Her dark curly hair had been done up on top of her head for the wedding and was tumbling down now. He couldn't help thinking it made her look as if she'd just come from a man's bed. That thought was followed by a white-hot flash of desire, which he quickly pushed away.

He had learned a long time ago that it was easier if he didn't think about Rosie that way. Most of the time he succeeded. Then, out of the blue—bam!—those feelings zapped him like a lightning bolt.

Nick had never said the exact words, but he had still made it clear that Steve was to think of her as a kid sister. That made her "hands off." He had taken his protective role to a new level today, he thought. After what he'd done, she wasn't going to any man's bed, including his.

Especially his.

"Why did you do it?" she asked. "You could have said no."

"To your mother?"

"No. Xena, Warrior Princess. Of course, my mother. When she asked you to submarine me, you could have told her you wouldn't stoop that low."

She was right. But he couldn't manage to summon the guilt he knew he should feel. He had absolutely no regrets. He'd built a booming business and had made a lot of money by giving his corporate clients all the information they needed to keep from making a mistake. He'd never taken as much satisfaction from a job well done as he did now.

Rosie was a one-in-a-million woman.

She didn't know it now, but she was better off alone than she would have been married to that two-timing jerk. Confronting Wayne without laying a hand on him had been one of the hardest things Steve had ever done. He'd wanted to punch Wayne's lights out, especially when he'd started spouting lies about Rosie.

"Look, squirt, you know why I couldn't say no."

"I don't." She shook her head. "It's easy. You open your mouth. It's one tiny syllable. 'No.' Simple."

"I owe your parents more than I can repay in a lifetime."

"You already paid off the college loan," she said. "With interest."

"It's not about money."

"Okay. It's about how when you were a kid my father caught you stealing from his restaurant and instead of calling the cops, he made you work."

"You got it."

She put her hands on her hips. "That doesn't make you my parents' lackey."

He couldn't help smiling. "'Lackey'? Rosie, you've been reading too many books in that store of yours."

"I'm serious, Steve. Maybe you like the word 'flunky' better? My folks gave you a helping hand. You don't owe them your life's blood forever. Your success is the only reward they want."

He owed them everything. "I know they don't expect anything."

"But you sided with them."

"I didn't take sides, and it's not a you-against-them situation."

"No?" She caught her full bottom lip between her teeth.

The longer she talked, the more he thought maybe she'd already gotten the waterworks out of her system. He studied her. She didn't look as though she'd been crying. Her turned-up nose wasn't red. No blotches on her face. No wadded up tissue in her hand. Nope, the storm was still gaining momentum.

She looked troubled. And angry. Hell, why shouldn't she? He'd just busted up her wedding. She would get over it. He took heart from the fact that when she'd listed everything she liked about Wayne, she'd never said she loved him. Although he didn't like to think about it, she wouldn't be alone for long. He hoped she chose the next guy more wisely. A girl like Rosie deserved the best.

"You've ruined everything," she said, taking her makeup case from the bathroom and setting it on the love seat.

He stuck his hands into his jeans pockets. "It may seem that way now, but give it time. You'll see—"

"All the time in the world won't change what you've done. You've destroyed my life," she said, her voice tight with suppressed resentment and simmering panic. "You and my mother."

He wanted to say he'd saved her life, but she wouldn't see that now. He almost wished he had come up empty when he'd checked out her fiancé. What he'd found was worse than he'd expected. In fact he'd kept the sleazy information to himself for a hell of a long time, hoping he wouldn't need it.

Then Mrs. M. had called him last night and told him about the wedding. He'd had to show her what he'd discovered. When she saw the information, paying Wayne off had been her mother's idea. The lesser of two evils was still evil, and he reminded himself that Rosie must be feeling pretty bad right now.

He tried to be gentle with her. "Your mother was concerned."

"My mother thinks Prince Albert wouldn't be good enough for me. You know that."

"She loves you, squirt. Your whole family does. They want the best for you."

"Who gets to decide what the best is? Shouldn't that be me? And when do I get to start calling the shots? I'm twenty-six years old. It's about time they stand back and let me alone. If I fall on my face, so be it. It's my face!''

And a nice face it was. But he couldn't tell her that. He didn't know what to say. Something positive. ''They're proud of you, Rosie.''

She shook her head. ''In a pig's eye.''

''Look at the bookstore. They're pleased at the success you've made of it.''

''That doesn't count. They couldn't force me into the family business and I used my trust fund to open the store. We're talking about interpersonal relationships here. My parents don't trust me, Steve. It's as simple as that. You don't interfere if you believe in someone.'' Her eyes turned accusing. ''And you of all people—I thought you would support me. You were the only one who didn't think I should go into the restaurant business with my brothers.''

She was right. He did a lot of work for the Marchettis. If she'd followed her brothers into the family operated restaurant chain, he'd have had to see her more than he could handle. He'd supported her desire to start her own business, but his motives had been selfish.

''I'm sorry you're upset,'' he said. ''But this is for the best. You'll see.''

''I'll never see that. And you helped do this to me.'' Her eyes got bigger—and angrier, if that was possible. ''You checked out Wayne, didn't you? You investigated his background.''

He nodded. ''When you first started seeing him.''

''Why? My mother?'' Her face was composed, even though she was mad.

''No one trusted him.''

Evasion. It was better than the truth. No way would

he tell her that no one had asked him. He'd done it on his own. She would want to know why and he wasn't sure he even knew the reason.

"I don't understand."

"Little things you said. No visible means of support, vague references to stocks and investments. He pushed his advantage with you at the speed of light." He was too slick, too smooth, too evasive. Too damn charming.

"So what did you find out?"

"Do you want to see the reports?" When had he learned to bluff so well? He prayed she would say no because he'd left them with her mother. Besides, he wouldn't show her everything. That info would devastate her. He'd agreed to do the dirty work, but he wouldn't destroy her in the process.

"Just tell me what you found," she answered.

He breathed a sigh of relief. "He lives off wealthy women."

"I don't believe it."

"Why would I lie?"

There was a bruised look in her eyes as she shook her head, indicating she didn't know. "But I'm not wealthy. That proves he cares about me for myself." She took a step forward, her eyes pleading with him to agree that she was right. "My bookstore makes a small profit, which Wayne encouraged me to channel right back into the business. Does that sound like a man after my money?"

"It sounds like a cheat who's done his homework." He walked over to her and nudged her chin up until her troubled gaze met his own. "How could he miss? Your family is well off. If he couldn't get it from you, he'd get it from them."

"So Mother commissioned you to cut to the chase."

He nodded. "He opted for the quick buck. And Flo figured the hurt you'd feel now is nothing compared to what it would be if you'd married that son of a—"

She put a hand over her mouth and turned away.

Here it comes, he thought. He figured action as the best way to deal with the situation. He would hurry her out of the hotel and to the airport and on the first plane back to California.

"It's time to go—"

"This is awful." She ignored him and started pacing. "You don't know what you've done."

"Yeah. I do. I got that cheating con man out of your life."

"I had to get married today. I *needed* to get married, Steve."

Something about the way she said "needed" gave him a bad feeling. "I don't understand. Define 'need.'"

When she faced him dead on, he didn't see the anticipated tears in her eyes. Just misery mixed with anger. And full-blown panic.

"I'm pregnant, Steve. I'm going to have a baby."

Chapter Two

Never say never, Rosie thought. Steve Schafer had finally noticed her.

If only it had been for her ravishing beauty, to-die-for body and irresistible charm instead of her shocking announcement. With all her heart, she wished that she could take those words back. Why in God's name had she blurted out her news like that? Her excuses lined up like ducks in a row: shock and hurt and anger, mixed with a down-and-dirty desire to shake him out of that damn complacency he wore like a pair of sexy jeans.

And fear. Terror had pushed the words out of her mouth.

She'd had the situation under control. She'd planned to marry Wayne and give her baby a name and a father. She'd been determined to make the best of their relationship. She would have made it work, too. But her well-meaning family, with Steve's eager cooperation, had raced to her rescue. Now she was out of the frying pan and into the fire.

Above all, Rosie did not want anyone else to know she was pregnant. At least not yet. But she knew she'd get more secrecy from a tabloid reporter than Steve. He'd been dispatched by her mother to take care of her; he would feel obligated to report that she was going to have a baby.

There were two reasons she didn't want them to know. Number one: she was afraid the shock would send her mother back to the hospital with another heart attack. Number two: she didn't think she could stand to see the hurt and disappointment on her parents' faces when they found out their only daughter had messed up so badly.

No. She had enough to handle without taking that on just now. Since she couldn't rewind and edit, she had to do some serious damage repair. But how?

"You're pregnant?" he said finally.

"Gotcha!" She pointed at him as she tried her best to grin, the last thing she felt like doing.

But turning it into a joke was all she could think of to do. How else could she make him go away? She needed to deal with the fact that her fiancé hadn't loved her enough to resist her family's meddling. Surprisingly, she didn't feel as if she was going to fall apart, but lately she couldn't tell. Her hormones were pretty whacked out. If she decided to have a good cry, she wanted privacy. The last person on earth she wanted to witness her breakdown was Steve Schafer.

"You're trying to tell me that was a gag?" he asked. He didn't believe her.

"Okay, it's not very funny. I'm not in an especially good mood. Put yourself in my shoes. How would you feel if I sabotaged your wedding?'' Did he know she was lying? She was no match for the man who put the ''cyn'' in cynical. He could see through anyone. But she wouldn't go down without a fight.

The look of pity on his face at the chapel had nearly been her undoing. If he knew about the baby, there would be a mega-dose of that expression and she would rather walk naked into a hailstorm than see it again.

Tension crackled between them and Rosie couldn't stand it. ''Next time, stay out of my life when my mother asks you to do her dirty work.''

Something crossed his face. A shadow. He almost looked guilty. Well, he darn well should. She was pregnant and not married. Thanks to him she never would be.

He folded his arms across his chest and leaned back against the cherrywood desk, looking far too comfortable, as if he were settling in for a heart-to-heart. A long time ago he had turned his back on her, given up his claim to soul-baring chats. He didn't need her, and she would never need him again. Lord, she wasn't feeling well. If her stomach decided to rebel, a frequent occurrence of late, she would never get rid of him.

''I'm not going to argue with you, Steve.'' How could there be arguing when she was the only one talking? The fact that he didn't rise to her bait and bicker back was immaterial, irrelevant, and completely unimportant. Not to mention frustrating and annoying. ''Actually, I'd like you to leave. Go back to my mother and tell her 'mission accomplished.'''

''I plan to go. But not without you. I have two plane tickets for Los Angeles, and we're going to use them. Right after we have lunch. It would be a shame to waste this food.''

"You eat. I'm not hungry." Why was he still trying to feed her? She folded her arms against her increasingly agitated stomach.

"You've got to have something. Since when do you turn down a meal?"

"Since I got stood up at the altar. A broken heart tends to put a girl off eating.''

He tensed. "I wish there had been another way. You know I hate this as much as you do.''

He really did look sorry. In fact, he looked terrible. Tired, as if he hadn't slept in days. She pushed the thought away. She'd give the man no quarter, no sympathy.

"You couldn't possibly feel like I do." He wasn't pregnant. And if he was, not only would it be a miracle, but there were any number of tall, leggy blondes who would drop everything to make an honest man of him.

"I wish things could have been different, squirt.''

"Yeah. Me, too.''

He looked apologetic, an expression just this side of feeling sorry for her. If he went to the pity place she wouldn't be held responsible for her actions. No jury of her peers—girls from interfering families who'd paid off a fiancé—would convict her for any mayhem she decided to wreak upon his decidedly hunky person.

"Why don't you try to eat? I got your favorites.'' In a single fluid motion he straightened and lifted the metal dome from one of the plates on the room service tray beside him. "Steak, potatoes au gratin, asparagus.''

She sniffed and her stomach lurched. Brought down by the smell! She put a hand over her mouth and raced to the bathroom, slamming the door. It didn't take long to get rid of the small amount of breakfast she'd been able to choke down. When she was steady, she rinsed her mouth out.

She was staring at her chalky-white face in the mirror when Steve knocked on the door.

Her humiliation was complete.

"Ro?"

"Go away."

"Are you all right?"

"Fine. Go away."

"Can I come in?"

"No. Go away."

The door opened. He took one look at her face, quickly but gently sat her on the side of the tub, and then wet a washcloth. He sat next to her and started to bathe her forehead and the back of her neck.

Even though she had ordered him out, she admitted to herself that the warmth of his body, the support implied by his actions, felt good. Too good. As much as she hated to admit it, this was more consideration than Wayne had given her since she'd told him about the baby. But at least he'd agreed to marry her. Now she had to get used to the fact that she was on her own. Thanks to Steve. She had to make him leave.

And she would. Real soon, she thought with a sigh as her eyelids drifted closed while he pressed the wet cloth to her forehead. "What part of 'go away' did you not understand?"

"When's the baby due?"

Her eyes snapped open and she pushed his hand

aside. "What baby? This was just nerves, delayed shock—"

"Look, I didn't just fall off the turnip truck, Rosie." He rested his wrist on his thigh and let the damp washcloth hang from his fingers between his widespread knees.

"And that means—what?"

"Wayne told me you were going to have a baby. I thought he was lying to get more money out of me. You really are pregnant, aren't you?"

She met his blue-eyed gaze for a few seconds, then nodded miserably.

He put his arm around her, ignoring her token resistance as he drew her closer to his side.

She rested her cheek on his solid, comforting shoulder, torn between wanting to push him away and needing to stay there forever.

"Before you ask, it's Wayne's baby," she said.

"I wasn't going to ask." He hesitated, then tensed. "Do you want me to find him? I'll—"

"No way." She pulled away from the security, shelter and warmth of his arms and stood. Retreating from him, she leaned against the sink. "It's just too pathetic. I wouldn't marry a man who took money from my family to break us up."

"Okay." He stared at her for several moments, then asked, "What are you going to do?"

"I thought I figured that out." She had the satisfaction of seeing him wince. "Now I'm not sure. Except for one thing."

"What's that?"

"I want this baby."

He nodded.

"I'm having it."

"All right."

"When my mother had her heart attack, she thought she was going to die. She told me how much she regretted not being able to see her grandchildren."

"She didn't mean for you to—"

"I know." She folded her arms across her waist. "I know. And she wanted me to be married. I didn't plan this, Steve. It was an accident. Sometimes things happen. Life throws you a curve. You can duck, or you can lean into it."

"You're going with it." He wasn't asking a question.

"I want this baby," she said again.

He nodded. "When are you due?"

"Six months." She knew what was going through his mind. Why hadn't she made plans to marry Wayne when she'd first discovered the pregnancy? That was none of his business.

But instead he asked, "Isn't morning sickness supposed to be over by now?"

She shrugged. "Marchettis never do anything halfway."

He nodded absently as he studied her. He was still sitting on the side of the tub. His intense gaze rested on her abdomen, assessing her for proof of the baby's existence. She felt like roadkill, but outwardly there was no sign. And she would know. Every day she looked in the mirror at her almost-flat tummy. Part of her couldn't wait to see how she would look, know what the baby's initial tiny movements would feel like, experience a good solid kick for the first time.

There was another part of her that hoped no one would notice for a decent length of time. By then she would have been married to Wayne and no one would have started counting back the months. Even if they had, it wouldn't have mattered because she would have had a husband. And the baby, a father. It had been a lovely fairy tale, one she realized that her shallow fiancé would have destroyed pretty quickly. But if Steve hadn't been so eager to take orders from her mother, at least the baby would have had his father's name.

After her parents, her brother Nick would take this news hardest. He had always been protective of her. Steve, too. His gaze lifted from her tummy, past her breasts, to her lips, where it lingered for a moment before he looked into her eyes. She saw an expression—something sad?—that made her want to wrap her arms around him. Before she could name the emotion, it was gone. Just as well. More than once she'd been accused of trying to mother the world. In a matter of a few months, she would be a mother for real. She needed to focus on her baby. His welfare came first.

"Six months isn't very long." Steve stood and let out a long breath. He ran a hand through his hair, then checked his watch. As he walked out of the bathroom he said, "The sooner your mother knows about this, the better. Are you packed? We've got a plane to catch—"

"You go ahead," she called after him.

He poked his head back in. "What?"

"I'm not going home."

Steve stared hard at her as he struggled to tamp down his frustration. Even more than before he wanted to get her to her mother. He wanted the peace and serenity of the Marchetti family cabin in the San

Bernardino Mountains. He wanted to forget his part in this mess.

He cursed Wayne for the umpteenth time. If he hadn't been world-class scum he wouldn't have taken the bribe and everything would be fine. But the weasel's cheerful greed had made Steve's dirty mission easy. He wished for five minutes alone with the jerk right now. But Rosie's fiancé was gone. Steve's work here was done. It was over. He could leave. All he had to do was take one of those plane tickets and split—out the door. Hit the road. As quickly as the thought entered his mind, he dismissed it. No way could he walk out on her. Not now.

Her pregnancy changed everything.

The situation had all seemed so simple when he'd left Mrs. M. It was all about getting Wayne out of Ro's life.

Rosie's baby put a one-eighty spin on everything. She was angry at her family right now. But she needed them. Somehow he had to convince her to go home to her mother. But the stubborn expression on her pale face told him he was in for a rough sell.

"If you don't go home, what will happen to your business? You have to get back to that. It's even more important now, with—" He made a vague gesture in the general direction of her stomach.

"A child on the way?" Her mouth turned up in a brittle smile. "Yes, I know. I'm not abandoning my bookstore. It's covered. I'd planned to take off two weeks for a honeymoon. Jackie is minding things there."

"What are you going to do?"

"Just take some time alone to sort things out."

"Your mother could help you do that."

"Then I wouldn't be alone. Besides, I don't need help," she snapped. "I'm a grown woman."

No kidding. He had tried on numerous occasions to ignore that fact, but her lush curves and unbelievable femininity reminded him on an excruciatingly frequent basis.

"Everyone needs help from time to time," he said.

"Even you?" she challenged.

"Even me." The answer was automatic. But the truth was, he didn't need anything from anyone. Not anymore. If he ever did, there was only one person he would ask. Nick Marchetti.

Their relationship was his most precious possession. He had money now and could buy anything he needed. Nick had been there when Steve hadn't had a dime to his name. You couldn't put a price on a friend like Nick. Steve knew how his buddy would take the news of his sister's pregnancy. Not well.

He kicked himself for not revealing his incriminating information right away, before Wayne had taken advantage of Rosie. Keeping it under wraps had seemed like a good idea at the time. Steve had figured the weasel would trip himself up and she would give him the heave-ho. In fact Nick had told him she'd dumped Wayne. Obviously not in time. Steve knew he would never forgive himself for that. Although he still felt he'd done the right thing in breaking up the wedding. Letting her know Wayne could be bought off had been for the best. Now she would never have to see the damning pictures. But that didn't change the fact that she was pregnant and not married. Guilt settled on him like a stone. He was to blame for at least part of it.

When Mrs. M. had asked him to stop the wedding,

Steve knew he could have said no. Rosie was dead-on about that. If he had, she would be married now. It was his fault that she had no husband to give her baby a name.

He was in way over his head. He had to try just one more time to convince her to confide in her family. "Rosie, you have to tell your mother."

"No, I don't," she said.

Stubbornness and sensibility didn't necessarily go hand in hand, he thought ruefully. "Sooner or later she'll have to know. Your dad, too."

She was pacing in front of the wide, sheer-draped windows. "Then it will definitely be later."

"Be reasonable."

"All right. How about this? I'll go on my honeymoon. When I get home, I'll tell them Wayne is on a business trip. He'll just never come back."

"Your mother knows I paid him off."

"Good point." She started pacing again. "You could back me up when I say that he didn't take the money."

"Your mother would wonder why the check was cashed."

"Oh. Right." She tapped a finger against her lips as she walked back and forth, deep in thought.

"Come on, Rosie. Didn't anyone ever tell you honesty is the best policy?"

She stood still and met his gaze with her own troubled one. "Whoever said that didn't have to face Flo and Tom Marchetti and tell them she was going to have a baby without a husband."

"It'll be okay. Trust your folks—"

"You don't know what it's like."

"No, I guess I don't." He didn't know what it felt

like to face parents, period. "I only had to answer to a social worker."

"Oh, Steve, I didn't mean—" She reached a hand out, then let it fall. "I'm sorry."

He shrugged. "No big deal."

"It's just that I'll have to look my parents in the eye and watch their faces. I can't stand to see 'The Look.'"

"They love you."

"I know. That makes it worse. The Look only works when it comes from the people you love."

"It can't be that bad."

"A flogging would be easier. Bread and water for a month would be a walk in the park. The Look is the ultimate punishment."

"What look?"

"Disappointment." She sighed. "I let them down, Steve. Big time. Nothing I could have done would be worse than this. Their friends, whose sons and daughters have given them legitimate grandchildren, will know that Rosie Marchetti screwed up. My folks will blame themselves, try to figure out where they went wrong with me. They should have been better parents, stricter."

"You're blowing this way out of proportion."

She shook her head. "That's what I'll see in their faces. Their daughter, their best and brightest, is pregnant and has no husband. How can I tell them that? I can't stand to hurt them that way—" Her voice cracked and she clapped a hand over her mouth and turned away.

Here it is, he thought. Here come the tears. He should have known she wouldn't cry for herself, but

her family was something else. And he was still the
only one there. He curled his fingers into his palms.

"Rosie, don't—"

"I'm fine—" She stopped as emotion choked off
her words.

"This won't do any good," he said.

"I know. I—I can't help it—" The words were cut
off by a strangled sob that shook her shoulders.

"Damn."

He crossed the room in three strides. He put his
hands on her arms and turned her toward him. He felt
her reluctance to take the comfort he was offering,
then her eyes swam with tears and she covered her
face with her hands. She seemed to crumple against
him.

Her sweet, soft body snuggling in his arms felt better than he had ever imagined, and he'd imagined it
a lot. She was like a sister to him, he reminded himself. He had no right to be aware of her breasts
pressed against his chest and the heat that burned
through him. He should push her away. How long
could he stand having her in his arms without doing
more?

He gritted his teeth. As long as it took, he decided.
She needed someone now. Fate had put him there. He
would just hold her. That's all.

But he couldn't stop himself from rubbing his hand
up and down her back in a comforting motion. He
was unable to resist pressing her cheek more firmly
to his chest. It felt natural and right for his arms to
tug her closer, tuck her softness more securely to his
hard length. He took a shuddering breath, then released it. She just needed a shoulder. It was the least

he could do. She was his best friend's sister. But he tightened his arms just a fraction. For himself.

When her crying subsided to an occasional wet hiccup, he said, "They'll forgive you."

"I know."

"They love you."

"No doubt about it. And I love them."

"They would want to help you through this, Rosie."

"Of course they would. But The Look will always be there—in their eyes. I'd do anything—*anything*—to spare them this disgrace and embarrassment."

"Anything?"

"Short of murder and mayhem," she said, nodding miserably. "But there's no solution to this problem." She sniffled. "I need a husband. But husbands don't grow on trees."

"No," he agreed. "Not the last time I checked."

She pulled back a little and looked up at him, a wavery little smile turning up the corners of her mouth. "They don't fall off turnip trucks, either."

"Yeah, I try never to do that. It's not the fall that gets you, it's the bounce."

The sound she made was part sob, part giggle, but it was all victory, one that made him feel as if he'd won a marathon.

As he pulled her back into his embrace, her words sank in.

I need a husband.

Then she could face her family and friends without shame. He took half the blame for her situation. He owed her. He owed the family. There was a way to help them all. But it was a huge risk. He could lose the best friend he'd ever had, the only family he'd ever known.

But Rosie was a part of that family. Shouldn't he help her? She was Nick's sister. If Nick were in his shoes, wouldn't he do the honorable thing, the gentlemanly thing? Steve hadn't hung around the Marchettis all these years for nothing. He'd learned a thing or two. Rule number one: when one of them was in trouble, they were all in trouble.

He wasn't a member of the family, not by blood. More than once he had wished there was a way to change that. But in this situation, blood lines worked in his favor. He could do something for Rosie that none of the rest of them could. He had a way to get her out of this jam.

"I could be a husband," he said.

She glanced up at him and her eyes widened. Then she smiled, and her face lit up, and he understood about the glow of a pregnant woman. She looked so beautiful, for a split second his breath caught.

"That's funny, Steve."

He frowned. "What is?"

"The idea of you as a husband. Not as funny as the image of you taking a bounce off a turnip truck. But still pretty hysterical. Have you been into that bottle of wine that room service brought up?"

He looked offended. "Why?"

"You're the world's most confirmed bachelor. After Nick, of course. But still, I can't picture you getting married. You're not very good husband material."

"Is that so?"

"Yeah." She frowned. "I'll forget you brought it up."

"For Pete's sake, Rosie. I'm trying to bail you out here."

She frowned. "You've already done enough for me today. Butt out, Steve. Don't do me any more favors."

"Hear me out. You need a husband. I'm available. I'm applying for the job."

"I don't believe it. You're actually proposing?"

He released a long breath and nodded. "Yeah, it's an official proposal. I'm asking you to marry me, Rosie."

Chapter Three

Rosie knew her jaw fell and her mouth opened. But for the life of her, she couldn't make any words come out. There hadn't been many times in her twenty-six years when she was speechless. Off the top of her head, she could remember two. The day the pregnancy test told her she was going to be a mother. And the time she had gone to Steve's apartment unannounced. She'd been eighteen and certain she'd seen a look in his eyes that had convinced her he was attracted to her. He'd answered the door shirtless, followed by a beautiful blonde wearing nothing *but* said shirt.

On the one-to-ten shock meter, the proposal from Steve hovered close to twenty. She was completely and utterly stunned. Was he really and truly on the level?

"Say something," Steve prompted.

She took a deep breath and released it. "At the risk

of offending the cliché police, all I can think of is—this is so sudden.''

''Yeah, well, there's a lot of that going around.''

''You silver-tongued devil. You could turn a girl's head with flattery like that.''

''Quit joking, Ro.''

''Why? You are.''

''No, I'm not.''

''Yes, you are. And it's a good one.'' She pointed at him and laughed with an edge of hysteria to the sound that even she heard. Those darn hormones were acting up again. ''I almost believe you.''

''Believe it.''

''How can I? This is me. And you're you.''

''And your point is?''

''One of two things. Either you're trying to cheer me up because you feel bad about what you did.''

''That's only half true. I will never feel bad about getting Wayne the Weasel out of your life.''

She winced at the derogatory nickname.

''What's my second choice?'' he asked.

''Payback. This is your 'gotcha' moment. This is revenge. This is Lucy holding the football for Charlie Brown. As soon as I run to kick the ball, you'll pull it away and let me fall on my backside, or in this case, my face, point and say 'gotcha!' ''

He stood, walked over to the phone and picked it up. ''Concierge, please.''

Puzzled, Rosie walked over to him, standing at his elbow while he waited with the receiver to his ear. ''What are you doing?''

''I'm going to find out about getting a justice of the peace.''

''Now?''

Challenging blue eyes, intense and hard as steel, locked with her own. "Right here, right now."

Rosie pressed the button to disconnect him. "You've made your point."

"So why did you stop me?"

"Like I said before, this is so sudden." She looked up at him and her stomach got that fluttery feeling she always got with Steve. "I don't remember responding to your proposal, in the affirmative or any other way."

"Okay. Now that I have your attention. Will you marry me?"

"No."

His eyebrows shot up. "That's it? Just no?"

"Thank you, no?"

"That's not what I meant and you know it."

She did know. He was being very sweet. He deserved an explanation. Unfortunately she didn't have one. Partly because this was happening way too fast.

"I'm not sure what part of no you don't understand. It's a one-syllable negative response. Fairly easy to comprehend."

He folded his arms across his chest and fixed her with a narrow-eyed stare. "I get it. This is *my* payback for not saying no to your mother, isn't it?"

"That would be childish. I can't believe you think I'm that immature."

"There's no way to predict how a woman will respond under the best of circumstances. But after a fiasco like today—"

She sighed. "It's very sweet of you to offer to do this for me. I appreciate it a lot."

"But you don't believe I'm sincere?"

She wasn't sure what she believed. A state of shock

wasn't the best place to make a decision about putting oneself in a state of matrimony. "This is something I have to handle by myself."

"It's about your independence, right?" He looked out the windows for a moment. "You've proven that you're a grown-up. No one questions that. Part of being your own person is knowing when to ask for help, how to know when you can't do it alone. This is one of those times. You need a husband. I can be one."

"True. By definition you can be a husband. But have you really thought this through? Let's forget for a moment what I want or need. This is completely not fair to you."

"Don't worry about me. I'm a big boy. I know my own mind."

"Okay, big boy. What are we talking here? Lifetime commitment? Open-ended arrangement? Specific time frame? What?"

He paced to the sofa and stopped to look out the windows as he rubbed the back of his neck. "How about this?" he said, turning back. "We stay together until the baby is born. Then we figure out where we go from there."

"Renegotiate in six months?" She thought about that. It felt so cold and wrong to consider marriage in the same breath as negotiation, which, as far as she was concerned, was a euphemism for splitsville. The Big D. Divorce. Maybe she *was* too much of a romantic, but she couldn't help it. She'd cut her teeth on fairy tales, and that was hard to shake.

"I'm sorry, Steve. I just can't do this. Not to you."

"You're not doing anything to me. It was my idea,

remember? This is about you. This is a practical solution to your problem.''

"Practical? Be still my heart.''

"You know what I mean, Ro.''

Yeah, unfortunately she did. She'd always imagined blowing him away with her triple whammy: beauty, brains and body. But over the years she'd seen the women who attracted him and, invariably, they were her complete opposite. Tall, leggy blondes. The night she'd gone to his apartment Rosie had finally gotten the message. She would never be tall enough, or pretty enough, or skinny enough to steal Steve's heart. And she didn't even want to get into the hair thing. She didn't have the time, money, or inclination to make hers straight and golden.

She was what she was. She was okay with being short, curvy and brunette. She'd come to terms with her type. But she would rather face The Look from her parents than marry Steve because it was practical.

Rosie shook her head. "It's out of the question.''

"You're still worried about me?''

"Not entirely.''

"Did it occur to you that you would be doing me a favor?''

Her heart gave a little leap. Maybe she had jumped to conclusions. Maybe he did care for her. Maybe this wasn't merely a sensible solution. He could have feelings for her. Stranger things happened.

"How would this be a favor for you?'' she asked cautiously.

"Your parents.''

Rosie felt like a punctured balloon. Deflated. Her tiny bubble of hope collapsed. "What about them?''

"If you have a husband when you tell them about

the baby, it will save them anxiety. I'm in their debt, Rosie. If it wasn't for Flo and Tom, it's anyone's guess what my life would be like today.''

''So this is like that thing where you save someone's life and they own you forever.''

''Sort of. But I don't feel like I'm their lackey,'' he said with a fleeting grin. ''This is definitely payback. I owe them more than I can ever repay.''

''If you knew my parents the way you think you do, you would know that they'd never ask you to sacrifice yourself on their behalf.''

Her voice trembled on the last word and Rosie caught her lip between her teeth. She had experienced some low moments where Steve Schafer was concerned, but this had to be the world's-record, low-down, bottom-of-the-lake, slimy low. She would probably live to regret this, but a girl had her pride. She wanted to receive a proposal that in some way reflected his tender feelings about *her*. Steve was asking her to marry him for her parents' sake. It was too humiliating.

''I know you're sincere. Truly I do. I care about my parents, too. But they're tough. They'll get through this like every other crisis they've weathered. Together. My answer has to be no.''

''For God's sake, Rosie, be reasonable.''

''I think I'm being exceptionally reasonable under the circumstances. Let me ask you something.''

''Shoot,'' he said.

''What about love?''

''What's that got to do with anything?''

''It has *everything* to do with everything, especially marriage. It should be the reason two people tie the knot, jump the broom, get hitched.''

"I don't believe this." He turned away and paced in front of the windows, the same place she'd worn a path earlier.

Suddenly Rosie was exhausted. "Go home, Steve. I'm fine. Your work here is finished."

He stopped and looked at her. "I already told you, I'm not leaving without you."

"And I told you that I'm not going home yet." She practically collapsed onto the love seat as if to say, "And you can't make me." That's mature, she thought.

He sat on the couch at a right angle to her, his knees barely touching hers. Leaning forward earnestly, he rested his elbows on his thighs. It was such a profoundly masculine pose that she felt a tiny catch in her chest, a slight escalation in her breathing.

"It's the right thing to do," he said.

"By 'it,' I assume you mean marriage?" she asked.

When he nodded, she acknowledged that he must be serious. Would it be easier to believe if he were down on one knee? Then it hit her why she was so adamant about not marrying him. She knew better than to believe for even a second that his motives had anything to do with tender feelings for her. From the time she was a little girl following him and Nick everywhere, she'd believed he walked on water. He had always included her when her brother would have ditched her.

As a vulnerable teenager she'd believed in "happy ever after." She had imagined Steve Schafer asking her to marry him. He would go down on one knee, take her hand and look longingly into her eyes and "pop the question" because he loved her to distraction. The proposal fantasy had never once consisted of "Yo, babe, let's get hitched so I can make an honest woman of you."

Oh, she knew he hadn't said that. But that's the way it felt. From the moment he had brought up the subject of marriage, it had been a complete and profound violation of her girlhood dream.

"I just can't do it, Steve," she whispered before emotion choked off her voice.

He took her hands in his. "Look at me, Rosie." He didn't say another word until she finally raised her gaze to his. She prayed there were no tears in her eyes.

"I'm going to take a shot in the dark here," he began. "You never once said anything about being in love with Wayne. The logical conclusion would be that you were marrying him for the sake of the baby. I can give you and the child protection from gossip with my name. So, other than the fact that I'm not the father, how would marrying me be any different? At least you know I wouldn't take advantage of your family."

The baby. She'd been so caught up in being stood up at the altar, and what her family would think about her, she'd momentarily lost sight of why she had been there in the first place. Although she wouldn't admit it to him, Steve was right. She *had* been settling for Wayne. Even though she'd been determined to make it work for her baby's sake, she couldn't lie to herself about why she'd agreed to marry him in the first place.

But Wayne was gone now. Unless she did something, her baby would carry the stigma of illegitimacy. Not a very nineties way of thinking, but she couldn't help it. Maybe she *had* read too many books.

The need to protect her unborn child emotionally as well as physically was deeply ingrained and profoundly instinctive. Steve was offering her a way to do that. He was old enough to know his own mind and smart enough to know what he was doing. She'd given him ample opportunity to back out, and he hadn't. Why should she let her wounded pride get in the way of her baby's welfare?

Steve squeezed her hands, the pressure gentle and reassuring. "What do you say, Ro? Will you marry me?"

It wasn't a down-on-one knee proposal, but it was sweet enough to tug at her heart.

She nodded. "Yes, thank you."

A short time later, Steve stood in the back of the chapel with Rosie beside him. He had hustled her there before she could change her mind. After securing the necessary papers through the wedding chapel, he'd convinced Judge Forbes to add them to his list of couples to marry. Now they were awaiting their turn. The justice of the peace was just finishing and they were next.

Steve studied the top of Rosie's curly head as she leaned over to smooth nonexistent wrinkles from her denim jumper. Her hand trembled slightly. She had wanted to put her wedding suit back on and Steve had talked her out of it. Partly because she'd worn that suit for Wayne and Steve didn't want anything about that jerk to touch Rosie ever again. But mostly because he didn't want to give her time to think about backing out.

Now that they were here, he knew it wasn't about her. It was him. He wanted to do this before he heard the taunting voices of the guys he'd grown up with in the county home. He knew what they would say. Halloween was over. Who did he think he was masquerading as a respectable man with something to offer? He had a lot of nerve asking a nice girl like Rosie Marchetti to marry him.

Steve didn't know why this marriage was so important to him, he just knew it was what he had to do. The only thing that gave him pause was Nick. He had never come right out and told Steve to keep his hands off Rosie, but the message had always been there—loud and clear. Steve told himself that the reason he had Rosie in this chapel for ''I do's'' wasn't about wanting her. It was about helping her out of a jam. Once her brother understood the situation, he'd be fine with it. Besides, it was temporary at best. Soon the dust would settle and they could all go back to the way things were before.

He believed that because he had to.

Steve felt Rosie tense beside him and he focused on the scene in front of him. The bride and groom kissed, then thanked the judge. On their way out of the chapel the radiant couple, decked out in formal wedding attire, passed by Steve and Rosie, dressed in casual clothes. He noticed their curious looks. It didn't bother him, but he didn't miss Rosie's frown. He wanted to smooth it away. He wanted to fix the problem. He promised himself that from this moment on, he would do everything he could to ease her misgivings and self-consciousness. From now until the day he wasn't around.

''Chin up, squirt,'' he said, taking her hand.

A doubtful expression flashed into her big brown eyes. She'd looked a lot like that before dashing into the bathroom earlier to toss her cookies. He hoped she was all right. Gently, he tugged her along with him to face the judge.

"Miss Marchetti. Mr. Schafer." The man glanced from one to the other with an expression somewhere between suspicion and confusion.

"Judge Forbes," Steve said, then cleared his throat. "I suppose you're wondering what's going on."

"The thought had crossed my mind."

"We can explain," Rosie added, staring hopefully at Steve.

This was his gig. It was up to him to pick up the ball and run with it. "It's simple, Your Honor. I've come to my senses about this woman. I convinced her that marrying me is best for both of us. The details are inconsequential."

The judge nodded hesitantly. "So you're ready to get married this time?"

Steve nodded and looked down at Rosie. Her face was pale, her eyes looked bigger, darker, more doubtful than ever, and she'd caught her full top lip between her teeth. "We're ready," he said confidently.

"Good." The judge opened his book. "We're here today to join this man and this woman in marriage." He glanced at them. "May I have the rings?"

"Oh, God. Sorry, Your Honor," Rosie said. She looked nervously at Steve. "We don't have rings."

Her tone bordered on backing out. "Rings aren't necessary to get married, are they?"

The judge shook his head. "I just always ask."

"We'll get them later," Steve said to Rosie. "Let's do it, Your Honor."

"Do you, Steve Schafer, take this woman to be your wife?"

"I do."

"Will you promise to love her, honor and cherish her as long as you both shall live?"

Steve hesitated. It wouldn't be a lie exactly. He did cherish her. She was his best friend's sister and he would take care of her to the best of his ability while they were married and after it was over. "I will," he said.

That was easy, Steve thought. The roof hadn't fallen in. As far as he could tell, lightning hadn't struck anywhere near where they were standing. Now it was Rosie's turn.

"Rosemarie Marchetti, do you take this man to be your husband?" She waited so long to respond, the judge finally asked, "Do you want me to repeat the question?"

"I do."

"Rosemarie Marchetti, do you take—"

"No, Your Honor," she said. "I was saying 'I do' to the question," she said hurriedly.

"I see. Then will you promise to love, honor and cherish him for as long as you both shall live?"

"Do I have to commit myself to that time frame?" she asked hesitantly.

Typical Rosie. Honest to a fault, he thought with a smile. How would the judge answer? he wondered.

The justice of the peace looked taken aback, but managed to say, "It's best to go into a marriage with the intention of making it a lifetime commitment. But I've seen more than one bride—and grooms, too—get cold feet at those words. How about if we just say, love, honor and cherish, and leave it at that?"

"I will," she said with a small smile.

"Then I pronounce you husband and wife. Congratulations, Mr. and Mrs. Schafer. My boy, you may kiss your bride."

Steve looked at the man. Kiss Rosie? Hell, he hadn't even trusted himself to hold her when she cried. Now this bozo wanted him to kiss her? He glanced at the woman beside him who he had always made it a point to try to think of as a little sister. The frown was back on her face. If he didn't follow through with this tradition, she would be humiliated. It didn't make any difference if their audience consisted of one person or a hundred. He wouldn't hurt her for anything.

Steve half turned toward her and released her hand. Curving his arm around her waist, he pulled her slowly and gently against him, acutely aware of her trembling. Cupping her cheek in his palm, he stared into her eyes for moment.

"I mean this in the nicest possible way. Gotcha," he whispered before lowering his mouth to hers.

Steve felt her smile as their lips met and knew she trusted him not to let her fall on her face. He slipped his hand into the thick, silky strands of her hair, gently pressing the back of her head to make the contact more firm. When she put her arms around his waist, Steve felt the air leave his lungs. His heart kicked into triple time, sending the blood pounding through his veins. His physical reaction to her was instant, powerful, and painful.

This was a hell of a time to confirm something he had always suspected. Holding Rosie Marchetti, especially while he kissed her, was the best thing that ever happened to him.

And the worst.

Chapter Four

"Talk to me, Steve."

"You're not nervous about this, are you?" he asked, feigning disbelief.

Rosie glanced out the airplane window, then swallowed hard as her stomach lurched. She had no control over the attributes of pregnancy that continually kept her insides on a roller coaster ride, but she'd stepped on this plane of her own free will.

They were descending into LAX. The lights of the Los Angeles basin sparkled like gold dust. It was breathtaking, or would be if she was looking down from the top of a small hill. From where she was sitting, nothing was beautiful. She wanted her feet planted firmly on the ground—now!

She glared at him, ignoring the teasing light in his eyes that she usually thought was so cute. "You know good and well when it comes to flying that I'm the world's biggest coward. Take my mind off this. Distract me. Say something witty."

"Okay. How about those Lakers?" he asked. When she glared at him, he laughed. "What do you want me to say?"

"I don't know. How about 'what's the plan after we land'?"

"I'd planned to drive to the cabin in the mountains. I thought you knew your folks offered it to me."

She shook her head, trying to ignore the stab of pain his "I" instead of "we" remark caused her. Maybe he hadn't meant it that way. Taking a deep breath, she said, "I don't remember Mom mentioning it. But maybe she did. I had a lot on my mind."

The humorous glint in his eyes disappeared. "Is your car at the airport?" he asked her.

"No. Wayne and I took a shuttle." Good grief. She'd expected to come home Mrs. Wayne Wallace, start housekeeping with her husband and await the arrival of their baby. Instead, her last name was now legally Schafer, and they hadn't even discussed living arrangements.

Mrs. Steve Schafer, she thought, mentally trying the name on for size. How long before that fact stopped feeling surreal?

"I can drop you off at your apartment before I go up to the mountains," he said helpfully.

She hadn't figured to get an answer to her question quite so quickly. Her dreamlike state had lasted about a second and a half, before his reply made her face cold, ugly reality. She was now a "Mrs." but it was in name only. She'd interpreted his "I" remark correctly. They were married, but there was no "we" in the relationship. It was every man for himself. There was nothing couple-like about them.

Rosie wasn't even aware that she'd had those expectations until Steve stomped all over them. Obviously exchanging "I do's" didn't mean that his plans now included her. The flash of pain and disappointment surprised her. But if it took every last ounce of the little bit of strength she had left, he would never know that he'd hurt her.

Before she could say anything, the Fasten Seat Belts sign dinged and lit up. Then a grinding, metallic sound beneath her feet caught her attention.

She gripped the armrest so hard her knuckles turned white. "Oh, God—"

"That's the landing gear." Steve pried her fingers loose and took her cold hand into his. "It's real hard to set one of these babies on the ground without it."

"I know. I just wish they could do it more quietly. Any sudden noise makes me nervous. I'd feel so much better if I could see the flight crew. If I knew they were talking about where to go for dinner after work and not about emergency vehicles lined up on the runway, then I could relax, too."

"Has anyone ever told you flying is safer than driving your car?"

"Yes. I dated a pilot once." She had the tiniest feeling of satisfaction when he frowned at that. Then the look was gone and she figured she must have imagined it. "He said if anything is going to happen it would be at takeoff or landing. So, after a successful takeoff, I have the whole flight to worry about what could happen on the other end."

"Nothing is going to happen. Are you buckled up?"

She stared at him. "Did it occur to you that the juxtaposition of those two sentences does not inspire calm and confidence?"

Without responding, he leaned over and gave her seat belt a tug to make sure it was secure. His gaze lingered a moment on her abdomen, then he met her gaze. "Is that too tight? For the baby, I mean?"

"It's fine," she said, touched that he would think of that. Then as the plane descended, her stomach seemed to drop. "Oh, mercy," she said, while his hand tightened around hers.

Several minutes later the plane touched the ground. Steve nodded with satisfaction. "One bounce. Not bad."

"No bounces would be better. And why do I always feel like I want to help put on the brakes?"

He just laughed as the plane taxied to the jetway. When they came to a stop, there was a flurry of activity as all the passengers stood and gathered their belongings. Rosie started to do the same.

"There's no rush. Let's wait," Steve said, putting his hand on her knee to stop her. "I don't want you caught up in the crush."

The heat of his touch on her leg seeped through the denim jumper and worked its way inside her, kick-starting the glow resting dormant in her abdomen. It took precious little to ignite the warmth. Rosie wondered what she could do to extinguish that little spark. It would help if he stopped being so sweet and protective.

"Aren't you in a hurry to get up to the mountains?" she asked.

"Not so much that I want you to get banged around," he answered, looking behind them at the passengers lined up in the narrow aisle. "They're jammed in here like sardines," he muttered.

The glow started again, or more likely it never

flickered out. How could he hurt her one minute, and the next do something so sweet she had an "ah, gee" moment that warmed her all over? But there was no need to spend energy and time on an answer because he obviously intended to dump her and head for the hills. Still, there were a few details they needed to work out before he left her to face her family.

The line of people finally began to move; in short order, the aisle was clear. Steve stood and moved to let Rosie precede him. She started to climb onto the seat so that she could reach the overhead bin where her carry-on had been stored.

"What are you doing?" Steve asked.

"Getting my bag. The flight attendant put it up here. Remember?"

"Would it kill you to ask for help, Ro? Let me do it."

What about when you're not around? Which obviously will be most of the time, she thought. Rosie patted herself on the back for *not* letting those words come tumbling out of her mouth. She didn't need him. He'd been kind enough to lend her his name, but responsibility stopped there. She'd learned to survive very well on her own. It would be best not to count on his help, as he'd made it crystal clear that he intended to be an absentee husband. Which suited her fine.

The thought rang hollow, but there was no time to think about that.

He reached up and grabbed the handle of her tapestry makeup case. As he did, the cotton material of his shirt pulled tight across his broad shoulders and strong arms. The play of muscles mesmerized her.

When she moved to take the bag from him, he

glared at her. "You're carrying this independent woman thing to the extreme, aren't you?"

"I'm perfectly capable of lugging my stuff. If you weren't here, I'd have to."

He didn't say it, but she saw a look flash into his eyes. She knew they were both thinking the same thing. If he weren't there, Wayne would have been. Steve was looking for some sign of how she felt about that. She wasn't sure. For a woman who'd had everything figured out a short time ago, she was pitifully unsure of anything now.

Steve stared at her. "While I'm here, you're not carrying anything heavier than a handbag." He set her case down long enough to shrug into his leather jacket.

Rosie wasn't sure if the masculine figure he now cut fully compensated her for covering up the view of his broad shoulders in that white shirt. But, she had to admit, either look was good.

She sighed, weariness overtaking her. Fatigue left her vulnerable. That had to be the explanation for her super-acute response to Steve. He was her honorary brother. She was immune to him. Any involuntary, visceral response to the contrary could easily be explained. She just needed more sleep.

"Okay, squirt, let's go."

'Nuff said. How could she possibly be attracted to a man who called her "squirt" on an annoyingly regular basis?

They walked through the airport, down some stairs, and stepped onto the escalator to get to Baggage Claim. As they did, Steve kept his arm around her, shielding her from the crush of people in the busy terminal. A girl could get used to this, she thought, even an independent girl. The trick was not to let that happen.

When they finally found the big, silver carousel, Steve set her case down and settled in to wait for the luggage to start circling. As he stood there, arms folded over his chest, he played havoc with her senses. His aftershave made her heart flutter, the sight of him turned her legs to jelly, and if he said one more word in his wonderful deep voice, she couldn't be sure of maintaining anything resembling her dignity. He had said he was leaving. Rosie figured the sooner, the better.

She touched the sleeve of his jacket. The smooth leather covered his warm skin, but her imagination was on overdrive and her fingers tingled. "I'll wait for the luggage. There's no need for you to stay. Go on up to the cabin. You've earned a vacation."

He had a what-the-hell-does-that-mean look on his face, but only said, "I'll see you home first."

She shook her head. "Not necessary. I'll take a cab."

"Not on my watch."

"Your watch?" With an effort she kept her voice calm. "What does that mean? Am I some kind of military expedition? Search and destroy?" She didn't often display the legendary, passionate Marchetti temper, but she'd just about reached her saturation point with him. She didn't enjoy feeling like the family mess that he was cleaning up. Giving him a smart salute, she said, "At ease, soldier. Mission accomplished, sir."

"Knock it off, Ro. I didn't mean it like that."

"Of course you did." Her emotions ranged from impotent fury to blinking back tears. She took a deep breath as she struggled for control. "I'm grateful to you for bailing me out with the wedding. But I can handle things from now on. You don't have to stay with me."

"What are you going to do?"

"Go home and pick up my car. I don't need your help with that."

"Define 'pick up your car,'" he said.

"There's nothing to define. One usually needs a car if one is planning to go somewhere. I'm not staying in my apartment."

"Of course you are."

She put her hands on her hips. "I'm too old to be grounded."

"That's not what I meant—"

"Isn't it? Look, you're taking a vacation. I've arranged time off from the store. This is probably the last opportunity I'll have to get away for a long time. I intend to take advantage of it."

"Where are you going?"

"Up the coast, maybe."

"Maybe? So you don't even have a place to stay?"

"This is January, Steve. How hard could it be to find a B and B at the beach?"

Steve had focused intently on the fact that his job would be done once he got Rosie home. He'd neglected to take into account the fact that she had a mind of her own. A mind-set that dictated *not* facing her parents.

"This is me, Ro. You're postponing the inevitable. Sooner or later you have to tell your family what's going on."

"Can't argue with that logic. But wouldn't it make more sense to do it when my *husband* is with me?"

He didn't miss her emphasis on the word. By definition, that's what he was. He'd said vows giving him legal right to the title. But he'd been so caught up in keeping his husband-in-name-only status—translation: keeping his distance from Rosie—that he'd forgotten something. If she faced her family alone, the jig would be up.

But jeez, after kissing her at the ceremony, his temperature had gone off the meter. And he'd wanted badly to kiss her again. If he did, he would want more. Years of perfecting his big brother act would be down the tubes if he let his instincts take over.

Marrying Rosie Marchetti had put him smack-dab on that fine line between friendship and duty. Nick would have a fit when he found out what Steve had done. But as long as he complied with her brother's hands-off-Rosie rule, there was still a chance he could salvage his relationship with the best—the *only* good friend he'd ever had.

Steve was afraid the only way to follow that rule was to stay away from Rosie. But he knew if he walked out on her now she would take off alone. That was a bad idea, and he knew better than to try to talk her out of it. That left him only one option, an equally bad idea. But he didn't have a choice.

"Do you have warm clothes with you?" he asked. When she nodded, he said, "Then you're coming with me."

Steve led the way up the stairs to the spacious mountain cabin. He welcomed the cold, fresh air that filled his lungs and cooled his body. He had expected to make the drive alone. He'd been wrong. Rosie had slept the whole way, but he'd been painfully aware of her presence. Her sweet smell had filled his head and set his senses on edge. The scent of her perfume was forever branded into his consciousness. Wide awake or sound asleep, she drove him crazy.

He must have been nuts to bring her along. He might have been able to turn his back except for the look in her eyes when he'd said he was going on his own. He knew it was more than the threat to take off alone that had swayed him. It was that same don't-leave-me-out look she'd always worn as a child when he and Nick were doing something. He hadn't been able to resist it then, and Rosie had grown into a sweet, shapely, seductive woman. He sure as hell had his work cut out for him to resist her now. The whole setup was a recipe for disaster.

Why hadn't he listened to Rosie? After he'd told her she was coming along, her reaction had made it clear she'd taken offense at his words. To quote her, they didn't need to be joined at the hip to make everyone believe they were a couple. He grinned as he recalled her crack about "misguided macho posturing." No one in the family would know they hadn't spent the whole time together. But he just couldn't leave her at the airport alone. Mrs. M. had entrusted him with the responsibility of her daughter and he wouldn't do the job halfway.

If only he could convince himself that she was safer with him than she would be in another state. If he gave in to his attraction, he would hurt her. He would rather die than do that.

On the wide wooden porch, Steve fumbled with his keys to find the right one for the front door. When he had unlocked and opened it, he noticed Rosie's brief hesitation. Then with her shoulders stiff and her chin held high, she passed him and walked inside.

She flipped the switch just inside the entry and the living room flooded with light. ''Brrr. This place is freezing.''

Steve turned on the thermostat and heard the heater instantly ignite. ''It won't take long to get warm. You stay here while I go get the suitcases out of the car.''

''You don't have to ask me twice,'' she said.

When he carried the luggage inside, Steve noticed her bending over the circular, screened-in fire pit that dominated the center of the room. She set newspaper and kindling in the middle and lighted it with a long wooden match. She looked up as he set the suitcases down.

''So which bedroom do you want?'' she asked.

Steve blinked. For some reason he had expected— maybe it was more that he'd *wanted*—her to claim her wifely right to share a room. He would have turned her down, no doubt about that. But she acted as if nothing had changed because of their vows. That bothered him. It shouldn't have, but with Rosie, he'd learned never to count on ''could,'' ''would,'' or ''should.''

He folded his arms across his chest and looked at her. ''I thought you'd want the master bedroom downstairs.''

''No. I'm here by default. The folks gave you the place. I wouldn't dream of kicking you out of the best room, even if it does have that great Jacuzzi tub.''

Share it with me. The room, the tub, the bed—all of the above. The thought flashed through his mind. He wished it was from out of nowhere, but he knew it was a function of spending too much time with a woman he could never have. For half a second he was afraid he'd said the words out loud. But Rosie never looked at him as if he had alligators crawling out of his ears, so he figured the idea had stayed in his head where it belonged.

Tiredly, he ran his hands over his face, then met her gaze. "Are you sure?"

She nodded emphatically. "I'll use my old room upstairs," she said with a wide, bright smile.

She was mighty damn cheerful about sleeping alone on her wedding night. Why? And what the hell was he doing questioning it? Never look a gift horse in the mouth. He'd never understood that expression. If someone had checked that wooden sucker out, the political dynamics of the world could be very different today.

Steve knew he should be glad she was making this so easy. Instead, he couldn't tamp down the annoyance her indifference generated.

She put a log on the brightly blazing kindling. "You never told me what my mother said when you called her from LAX."

"Yeah, I did, before I realized you were asleep."

"Okay, I'll rephrase. What did my mother say when you talked to her?"

"I didn't talk to her. No one was home. I left a message on her answering machine and told her not to worry, everything was fine."

Her full lips twisted wryly. "That should put her mind at ease."

"She knows where I am if she wants details," he said, sitting on the bricks beside the fire. He watched Rosie nudge the blaze with the poker.

"Did you know that when my folks first bought this cabin it was one story?"

He shook his head. "It was like it is now the first time I came."

"They used it for a getaway place when Nick and Joe were little. After Alex and Luke and I came along, it was harder for them to leave us. But at least once a year Grandma Marchetti would come and stay with us kids while Mom and Dad came up here to be alone. When Grandma got older, there was no one they trusted to dump us on."

"'Dump'?"

"What else would you call it? No one cheerfully begs to watch five hyper children."

"I suppose not."

A pensive look wrinkled her forehead. "My parents just had a wedding anniversary."

"How many years?"

"Thirty-five. Mom got pregnant with Nick on their honeymoon. In this cabin." Her expression changed, turning somewhere between pleasure and pain.

"What is it, Ro?"

"Don't take this the wrong way, because it's not your fault. It's all my fault. I appreciate the sacrifice you've made—"

"Jeez, Ro, stop. I'm not some knight in shining armor."

"I can't think of anyone who would have done what you did. And I don't expect anything more. You've been a wonderful friend, Steve—"

"Are you going to continue to play the Queen of Qualifying or just spit it out?" He smiled. "What is it you're trying to say?"

"I just can't help being a little bit sad."

"About what? Specifically," he added at her pointed look.

"From the time I was a little girl, my mother always told me she hoped I would find a man as wonderful as my father. All she ever wanted for me was a long, happy marriage, like hers."

"You'll have that someday."

"Wish I was as sure. I've done everything wrong. It's a sure bet my parents' marriage of thirty-five years didn't start out like ours."

Steve wondered if she was already regretting marrying him. He couldn't blame her. A guy with his negative family credentials wasn't something a girl like Rosie could brag about.

"I suppose not," he said.

"My parents were in love."

He smiled. "Yeah. They still are."

She looked at him and the corners of her mouth lifted. "I know." Her smile faded. "I could be wrong, but I'm fairly certain Mom and Dad didn't start their honeymoon with a conversation about which bedroom the other wanted."

Steve figured it was a sure bet they'd shared a bed and everything that went along with it. Mr. M. still looked at Mrs. M. as if she hung the moon. He'd never seen his father and mother together; didn't know if they had even married. The Marchettis were together. As far as he could tell, they were pretty content, too. They were the exception. Steve figured a guy like himself had no business believing in happy endings. No way would he drag a girl like Rosie down with him.

"I always wanted to follow in their footsteps," Rosie said.

He didn't know what to say. "Your folks just want you to be happy."

She opened her mouth to say something, then hesitated. "I may not be following in their footsteps. But thanks to you, at least I don't have to tell them I'm pregnant and not married."

"I'm not so sure I've done you any favor," he said truthfully.

Chapter Five

A week later Steve was still convinced that he hadn't done her any favors. He prowled the cabin like a caged tiger, feeling like a thunderstorm about to explode. Talk about your mixed metaphors, he thought irritably.

He glanced at Rosie as she finished the breakfast dishes and hung the towel over the drainer resting on the ceramic tile counter. Even dressed in jeans and a sweatshirt, she looked domestic, maternal, serene—perfect. And so beautiful he ached. He was dopey, sleepy, cranky, crabby, and any of the other seven dwarfs who were not happy about sharing a cabin with a woman.

Nothing had changed since the night of their arrival when he'd hardly slept for thinking about Rosie. Their rooms were on completely different floors but still not far enough away. He couldn't seem to get her off his mind long enough to get a whole night's rest. He kept hoping sheer exhaustion would set in.

But apparently his need for her was stronger than mere basic survival instincts.

So much for isolation, peace and serenity. That idea had crashed and burned as soon as he'd knuckled and decided to bring Rosie with him. But there really hadn't been any other choice if he was going to protect her reputation. Marrying her had seemed simple. He was beginning to realize that he hadn't thought it through. He'd been so focused on protecting her from everyone else, he'd underestimated one detail.

Protecting her from himself.

Steve would rather cut off his right arm than hurt her. Calling this interlude a honeymoon, with all that the term implied, made him nervous. Not as nervous as being alone with her. He liked Rosie; he always had. Too much. And he didn't trust himself to keep his distance. She deserved someone with a background like hers, a guy from a big family who had learned how to be a husband and father. Some day, when her life settled down, she would find that guy, and Steve would do his best to be happy for them.

He stood in the living room, staring out the picture window at the spectacular view of mountains, pine trees and blue sky. A storm earlier in the month had left two feet of snow on the ground.

"Hey, tiger," she said, stopping beside him.

He jumped as if she were a covert operative launching an attack. "You should give a guy some warning," he growled.

"I thought I did. Who tweaked your tail this morning?"

Apparently she'd sensed his caged tiger attitude and was jumping into the milieu right along with him.

He rubbed a hand down his face and his stubble

rasped against his palm. "Sorry. I haven't been sleeping well."

"Remind me to fix you some warm milk tonight."

"Warm milk won't cure what ails me," he said under his breath.

"What?" she asked.

"I said, it's warm and the azure sky hails me."

"Since when do you wax poetic?" she scoffed. She looked out the window. "But it is a spectacular day."

Definitely spectacular, he thought. Wide, open, and space for a man to lose himself along with everything that ailed him. Big enough to get away from Rosie and take the edge off his need.

"I think I'm going for a walk," he said.

"What a wonderful idea."

He groaned inwardly. She wanted to come along. How did he tell her that he desperately needed to be alone to get a grip on his out-of-control emotions? That her coming along would defeat his purpose? That this was a "cold shower" moment?

Instead he said, "It's too cold for you."

"I'll bundle up."

"I thought you weren't feeling well. Morning sickness and all."

"I'm feeling better now. It seems to have settled into something like functional nausea. And I have a lot more energy."

"What about the altitude? Are you sure it's safe to exercise in your condition?"

"My doctor advised exercise. The fresh air would be wonderful. I didn't know that pregnancy was considered a physical limitation."

Then the sparkle in her warm brown eyes sputtered like a worn out lightbulb and flickered out. There it was, that don't-leave-me-out expression on her face. She looked as if he'd taken her favorite doll and stomped it into the mud. He could no more deny her than he could stop wanting her.

"Okay. But bundle up. Stragglers get left behind."

When his words sank in, she smiled, and the radiance took his breath away.

"Last one out is a rotten egg," she said, grabbing her jacket from the closet by the door.

Steve reached for his parka, then left it, figuring the cold would bring down his body temperature if not his libido. That was something, at least. It should do the trick. After all, by definition, the wide open spaces wasn't big on privacy. What could happen?

Rosie's low-topped boots clunked on the wooden deck and stairs as they descended to the walkway in front of the cabin. As if by mutual consent, they bypassed the snow-plowed road that meandered past the other cabins on Blue Jay Lane, and headed into the woods. The fresh, pine-scented air felt wonderful on her warm cheeks. Moving around drove away her lassitude. She wasn't sure what had changed his mind about letting her come along, but she was grateful. Being with Steve always put her in a good mood.

In silence, they walked at a steady clip. He was moving fast, releasing some pent-up tension, she sensed. Or maybe it was just a guy thing, that need to focus, even if it was just a leisurely walk. Already slightly breathless, she wondered how much longer she could keep up with him. If the pace quickened any more, he would leave her in his dust or, in this case, a snowdrift.

Rosie cast a covert glance in his direction, then almost wished she hadn't as her breathlessness hiked up a notch. The increase had nothing to do with the exercise, and everything to do with Steve. He reminded her of a lumberjack, born to the woods. Dressed in boots, worn jeans that intimately hugged his muscular thighs, and plaid flannel shirt over his thermal top, he cut a masculine figure.

Darn it, she hated when that happened. From out of the blue the attraction hit her. She didn't want to be aware of him, not in a man/woman kind of way. Every time she did, her heart was left bruised and battered. She should have stood her ground in the airport and not let him convince her to come along with him.

It was bad enough that she had given in to his convincing rationale against her instincts of self-preservation. But now, after a week of being cooped up with a man who acted like a bear, she was walking by his side. On top of that, she was noticing that Steve Schafer would give the current Hollywood heartthrob a run for his fan club. Could disaster be far behind?

Rosie shivered and stuck her hands into the pockets of her jeans. They were tighter than she'd noticed them being a week before. Her figure was changing to accommodate the baby. That's where her focus should be.

"You warm enough?" he asked, frowning at her.

She nodded. "You?"

"Yeah," he said with more enthusiasm than she felt the temperature warranted. "You tired?"

"No way." She glanced at him. "You?" she asked, wondering if he heard the hopeful note in her voice.

"Nope."

They kept going in silence for a few more minutes.

He glanced over at her. "Am I walking too fast?" he asked.

"Of course not," she said, trying to hide her huffing and puffing. There was no way to camouflage the white cloud of her breath between them. "Why do you ask?"

"No reason." One corner of his mouth turned up. "It's just that we're in Smokey the Bear country. Someone might mistake that smoke screen in front of your face for a forest fire."

"Cute, Schafer, real cute."

He slowed down. "This isn't a race."

"Don't do me any favors." She sucked in air. "I can keep up."

"I know you can. But I'd appreciate it if you could cut me some slack. I'm not used to the altitude. It's been a long time since I've been up here."

"In that case," she said magnanimously, "I'll ease up on you."

"So that's how you want to play it?" There was a glint in his eyes, putting her on notice that he would do something.

Resting his hands on his knees, he bent as if to catch his breath. With the grace, agility and speed of a big cat, he leaned down, and picked up a handful of snow. Before she could react, he'd tossed it at her, hitting her squarely in the face. She gasped at the cold and her cheeks tingled.

"You're dead meat, Schafer."

Rosie grabbed a snowball and hurled it in his direction. He ducked and the frozen missile arced harmlessly by his ear.

He grinned. "You never could hit the broad side of a barn, Ro."

She put her hands on her hips and feigned indignance as the blood sang in her veins. Exhilaration bubbled through her and she couldn't remember the last time she'd felt so alive.

"This is war, Schafer. I'll give you one chance to say uncle, then all bets are off and I show no mercy, take no prisoners."

He laughed and shook his head pityingly. "Misguided spunk. I like that about you, Ro."

"Squirt is bad enough. But never under any circumstances call me spunky."

"I'll consider myself warned."

"So you're not going to surrender?" she asked.

When he shook his head, his conquering-hero grin widened. How many women had fallen at his feet on account of that smile? Insufferable man, she thought. She would show him. "When your male ego is trounced into a whimpering, bleeding mass in the snow, don't say I didn't warn you."

"I won't. Usual rules?" he asked.

She nodded. "There are no rules."

He loped off through the trees and Rosie knew he was gathering ammunition for guerilla warfare. She needed to find a snowbank to defend and stockpile her own arsenal. When she was ready, she peered into the woods, watching and waiting, her heart beating hard in anticipation. Soon she caught a glimpse of his blue-green plaid shirt as he skulked from tree to tree, trying to get around behind her.

She shifted her position, always keeping the mound of snow between them. Finally, she heard his rendition of a Confederate yell as he broke through the woods lobbing snowballs in her direction. The small hill protected her. When his stores were used up, she launched her own attack. But to hit him, she had to get in closer.

She chased him down and made several direct hits. With four snowballs left, she tossed them at him one after the other, until his shirtfront was dripping and his wet hair hung in his eyes.

"Are you ready to admit defeat?" she asked.

"Okay," he answered. But she didn't trust the way he held one hand behind his back.

"You haven't said uncle yet," she reminded him.

For every step he took toward her, she moved back an equal distance. When a tree stopped her retreat, Steve pounced. Her parka was unfastened. She squealed as he stuck a handful of snow down the front of her sweatshirt. Suddenly his feet slipped and he went down into the soft snow on his back. Rosie went with him and landed on top.

He was breathing hard and clouds of white filled the small distance between their faces. Their lips nearly touched. His blue eyes went from teasing to intense in zero point four seconds. Rosie was sure he could feel her heart pounding. More than anything, she wanted to know what his kiss would feel like. Just once. She knew if she ignored this chance, she would regret it as long as she lived.

She lowered her mouth to his.

His lips were soft and warm. He tasted of coffee and fresh air and snow and especially surprise. When she pulled away and stared into his eyes, Rosie knew she'd made a big mistake. This was going to be another in a long list of humiliating moments where Steve Schafer was concerned.

Steve struggled to control his emotions, which were fast escalating out of control. His first reaction was confirmation of what he'd always suspected. Holding Rosie in his arms was about as close to heaven as he ever expected to get. He wanted more. He sensed himself standing on the edge of a steep bluff. If he made one false step, he'd go down and there would be no way to stop the downward slide, no way to save himself.

He'd known about Rosie's girlhood crush on him. He'd have had to be deaf, dumb and blind not to be aware of it. As he stared into her big, beautiful, brown eyes he wondered if she still harbored any of those feelings. He couldn't help hoping. But he knew better than to believe a woman could love him. Wanting was something else. Desire he recognized and understood. Seeing it on Rosie's face struck a corresponding chord in his own soul. At the same time, he saw that she was scared and unsure. That was his undoing.

When she started to lever herself off him, he tightened his arms around her. He raised his head, touching his mouth to hers. At that moment he forgot that he was wet and cold, ignored his need to distance himself from her, and overlooked the fact that she was off limits to him.

Nothing mattered but the feel of her breasts pressed against his chest, the warmth of her body intimately snuggling into his, and her ragged breathing that matched his own.

Their mouths never parted as he rolled them onto their sides, cushioning Rosie with his arm as he held her. They were creating enough heat to melt the snow around them. Steve struggled for restraint as the flash fire of passion raced through him. Desperately he fought for control as Rosie snuggled trustingly against him. He'd wanted her for so long.

Instinct took over and he surrendered to her temptation. He couldn't raise the will to stop himself as he cupped her breast in his palm. Supreme male satisfaction spread through him when she moaned then wiggled herself more intimately into the touch.

Steve nibbled her full top lip and heat surged through him as her mouth opened to welcome him inside. Her tongue mated with his as they mimicked the consummation that their bodies yearned for.

Her curves beckoned, and he slid his hand down her hip and thigh, then back up to her waist. When his fingers stopped at the snap of her jeans, she sighed and exhilaration poured through him. A twist of his fingers unhooked the closure. He started to do more and she shivered. That stopped him cold. He went still.

What the hell was he doing?

He sat up.

"What's wrong, Steve?"

"You're cold. Let's go back to the cabin before you catch cold."

"But—"

He got to his feet, and pulled her up, too. "No buts. Pneumonia wouldn't be good for you—" he glanced down at the open snap of her jeans "—or the baby."

Without giving her an opportunity to protest, he took her arm and headed them back to the cabin. Her hurt and confusion was almost tangible, but he knew this was for the best.

He chanced a glance at her, then wished he hadn't. His heart caught, she looked so beautiful, sexy, like a woman who had just made love to a man. Her silky hair was a riotous mass of curls bracketing her rosy cheeks. A frown drew her dark brows together, and there was a bruised look in her eyes.

God, how could he have been so stupid? He was despicable, the lowest form of existence. For all his noble intentions, the first time he got close to her, he'd done what he'd promised himself he would never do. Not only had he kissed her, he'd touched her with every intention of doing more. If her shiver hadn't brought him to his senses, he'd have a hell of a lot more to be sorry for. So much for safety in the great outdoors.

It would never happen again, he promised himself.

Four days after kissing Steve—the biggest mistake of her life—Rosie had never felt so lonely in her life. He'd hardly spoken to her since. He either buried himself in books, or went out for walks. There wasn't any question of her going along since he never invited her. She'd always thought the phrase "passive aggressive" made no sense. But his silent treatment screamed loud and clear that he hadn't much use for her.

She thought about the philosophical question of whether or not a tree falling in the woods made noise. Putting her own spin on it, she wondered if there was any sound when a woman kissed a man in the woods.

"Just the crack of my heart," she said to herself.

This was just too pitiful, she decided. They had three more days before it was time to go home and face the family. She would have to grow some gumption then, so she might as well start now. She would not sit around and "poor me" herself for what would never be.

She glanced across the living room where Steve was hiding behind the latest hardback techno-thriller.

"Steve?"

"Hmm?" he said, not looking up.

"I'm going stir crazy. Would you mind if I borrowed your car and drove into the village?"

The book lowered and he stared at her. "They're predicting snow for the mountains."

"Not till later tonight. I'll be back before then."

He slammed the novel shut. "I don't think driving is such a good idea. The roads are pretty slick."

"You're worried about your car." She headed for the telephone. "I'll call a cab."

He sprang out of the chair, then crossed the room and stopped beside her. "I'm concerned about *you*."

Yeah, and the moon is made of green cheese, she thought. If he cared at all for her, he wouldn't treat her like a West Point cadet who'd been caught cheating on a test. She now had firsthand experience with how well the silent treatment worked as a punishment.

She took pride in the fact that she hadn't voiced those thoughts. Especially since she couldn't hold him entirely responsible. After all, she was the one who had kissed him. Everyone was entitled to one mistake. But if you did the same thing again, it was cause for induction into the moron hall of fame. That was a place she had no intention of going. Steve would never have one single inkling that she had any feelings for him other than gratitude and friendship.

"Don't worry about me. I'll be fine." She pulled out the directory and opened it to the page for cab companies. "My name will be mud if I don't bring back something for my mother."

Before she could look through the Yellow Pages, he shut it. "I'll drive you into town."

"That's not necessary. Keep enjoying that book. I'm capable of getting to and from town on my own."

"You can bring Mrs. M. a souvenir, but if I don't bring her *you,* my name will be worse than mud."

Before any warm fuzzy had a chance to form over his protective instinct, she reminded herself that he was nothing more than her bodyguard. Warmth of the unfuzzy, very sexy kind flashed through her as she remembered him touching her body in ways that had nothing to do with guarding. Her cheeks burned at the thought. The best method she'd found to combat his appeal was anger, but it was hard to stay mad when he was so sweet. Until they could discreetly disentangle themselves from this situation, she would have to do something to get over her weakness for him. Somehow she would have to get the message to her heart that Steve never had and never would care about her the way she wanted.

She opened her mouth to say something and he touched her lips with his finger. "Look, Ro, we can stand here and argue about this if you want. But time's awastin'. Here's the bottom line: you'll never get past me. I'm bigger, stronger, tougher, and you are *not* taking a cab or driving slippery roads by yourself. Period."

He was being sweet again. Rosie suppressed the painful direction that thought would lead her and forced a smile. "All right, lackey. You can come."

He grinned and she turned away before that charmingly boyish look could do her too much damage.

A short time later they strolled down the village's snow-lined street dotted with shops displaying engagingly decorated windows. There were more people than she would have expected on a Friday; she figured they must be getting a one-day jump on the weekend. The clouds overhead and a brisk wind made it bitterly cold and Rosie pulled her jacket more snugly around her.

"Let's go in here," she said, pointing to a store with knickknacks displayed. "Mom always liked this place. It's got everything from shelf paper to fashion accessories. Maybe I can find something for her in here."

"Okay."

Steve opened the door and waited for her to go inside.

Her gaze was drawn to a long wall filled with children's things. The plush stuffed animals drew her like a magnet. She picked up a rag doll and fiddled with the yarn hair and floppy arms. "I had one just like this when I was a little girl," she told Steve. "I still have it somewhere, thanks to you."

"Me?" He stuck his hands into his jeans pockets and leaned a broad shoulder against the wall. "You're on thin ice here. I never played with dolls. Any hint of impropriety in that regard would create a ripple of shock through macho men everywhere."

"Kind of like 'The Force'?" When he nodded, she grinned. "Tell me you don't remember rescuing Gwendolyn from my brother Joey before he could pull off the other leg. Then you strong-armed him into telling you where he'd hidden the amputated limb so you could fix it."

He shook his head. "I have no independent recollection—"

"You're lying," she accused. "Deny it if you

want. It's enough that I remember.'' Then she sighed. ''I have so many wonderful memories of growing up.''

''You're lucky.'' He folded his arms across his chest.

She glanced at the infant sleepers beside her. ''I hope I can give my baby a happy childhood.''

''That phase of life is highly overrated.''

His sharp tone caught her attention. She studied the tight jaw, the lines that deepened on either side of his mouth, the hard look in his blue eyes. He *had* put the ''cyn'' in cynical, but she supposed he had reason. She'd like to give a piece of her mind to the parents who had thrown him away as if he were nothing more than a rag doll. Even more, she'd give anything to take away his pain.

Life was hard enough without starting out alone. She had her parents and brothers. Their interference annoyed her, but she knew their motivation was love. Her baby wouldn't have a father, but she would be around. There would be uncles and grandparents. Steve had given them a cover story to explain any future questions about parentage. She wished she could give him something back.

''I think you started M.M.A.''

One corner of his mouth lifted. ''Macho Men of America? How do you figure that?''

''You had to do something to camouflage your soft heart.''

''A vicious rumor.''

''Then explain the plaque in the cabin kitchen and the events that followed.'' When he shrugged indicating he hadn't a clue what she meant, she said, ''Work with me here, Steve. Walk backward through your mind. My father took the rest of us fishing while you stayed behind and hung that plaque for Ma. When you joined us at the lake, Nick made fun of you for helping a chick. I pushed him in the water.''

He smiled. ''Okay. Then he got even and did the same to you and you almost drowned.''

''But you pulled me out.''

His smile faded. ''It wasn't macho. I just got lucky.''

She shook her head. ''I'm the fortunate one. But I bet you wish you hadn't been so quick that day.''

''Why would I?''

''Then you wouldn't be stuck married to me now.''

Chapter Six

Steve was mad as hell. The reminder of that day and the fact that she could have been ripped out of his life forever sent cold chills down his spine.

He stared hard at her. "I don't regret marrying you any more than I regret pulling your behind out of the lake that day. Don't you ever say anything like that again."

"Lighten up. I was joking."

"It wasn't funny," he said, an edge to his voice.

He knew he would never be sorry, not for one second, that he'd married her. He knew it as surely as he knew he could only stay with her until she didn't need him anymore. Rosie deserved a better man than him. Her brother had always known that.

"My mistake," she said, studying him intently.

He glanced at the baby paraphernalia beside him. "Look, if we're going to get a souvenir for Mrs. M., I suggest we try a different department."

Steve followed her around the store, struggling to

control the maelstrom of feelings Rosie had stirred up. The intensity of his reaction to losing her startled him and shook him to his core. He wished he was alone with his book, taking cover behind it. Fat lot of good that would do him.

In the past four days, he hadn't retained a single word he'd pretended to read. But short of skipping out on her, it was the best he could do to keep his distance, and his feelings for her, under control. Unfortunately, it had worked about as well as a cold shower, his stroll with her through the woods, or anything else he did with Rosie nearby.

He still wanted her.

Steve hated shopping, almost as much as he'd despised his childhood. Rosie brightened up this tedious experience the same way she had brought sunshine into his life from the first time he'd seen her. He still enjoyed watching her.

She wandered around the shop and picked up a set of candlestick holders. The glitter of the crystal ran a distant second to the sparkle in her eyes. She read funny cards, and her merry laugh made him smile. When her gaze was drawn again to the tiny baby bibs and blankets, her face filled with emotions that he couldn't name. He wanted to pull her into his arms and reassure her. She would be a good mom. No way would she turn her back on her kid.

It didn't surprise him when she picked out something for her own mother in that vein. She finally chose a wooden plaque that read "Mom's busy. Pick a number. Line forms to the right. No problem's so big it can't be fixed with a hug."

They left the store, and Rosie pulled her purchase

out of the bag to study it again. "Do you think she'll like this better than the candlestick holders?"

"She'll love it."

"How can you be so sure?"

"Because it's from you."

Rosie's eyebrow lifted. "You're tired of shopping, aren't you?"

"Nope. I'd like nothing better than to spend hours in there," he said, indicating the store they'd just left. "But I think we should grab a quick, early dinner and head back to the cabin before the weather turns."

"You're good, Steve. Most women wouldn't be able to tell that you're bored to tears."

"No way. Did you see tears? I don't think so. It's in the M.M.A. rule book, right up there at the top. Number one or two. 'Macho men do not cry, for any reason.'"

"Sell it somewhere else, Schafer. I've got your number."

"Okay. I'll buy your silence with dinner. Anywhere you want."

Without hesitation she said, "The Hot Dog Hut. Sauerkraut, relish, mustard and onions."

"Lucky for me your silence comes cheap."

Her smile warmed him inside and out, touching the dark place in his soul that only she'd ever been able to reach. He was in big trouble. He could feel it. He was afraid no book in the world, paper or hardback, would be enough to protect him from Rosie Marchetti. Definitely Marchetti, not Schafer. He couldn't, wouldn't, think of her as his wife. If he did, no power on earth could protect her.

Steve ushered Rosie through the cabin door and felt her shiver. "It's cold in here. I'll build a fire," he offered.

"That sounds wonderful. While you do that, I'll whip up some hot chocolate."

When she came back with a couple of steaming mugs, Steve had a blazing fire going. She held out a cup to him, then sat on the brick seat beside the fireplace and leaned toward the warmth. "That feels so good."

"It's pretty cold outside."

"On the radio, the weatherman said reports of snow were greatly exaggerated."

"Yeah." Good thing, too, he thought.

He'd hate to get snowed in up here. It was Friday. They'd leave for home early Sunday. All he had to do was get through one more day. That was doable.

Even if his will power was wearing mighty thin.

Even if all he could think about was Rosie.

Even if he wanted to kiss her again, and touch her again and make love to her.

A little over twenty-four hours and they would be outta there. Then she would be safe from him.

He put his mug down. "I think I'll hit the sack."

"But it's early," she said, a hint of hurt in her voice. "I can only guess what the macho men's rule book would say about *that*."

Steve hated the disappointment in her tone, hated that he'd put it there. But he couldn't help admiring her attempt at humor to cover it. That still wasn't enough to change his mind to stay there with her in the most romantic setting he could imagine. But he made the mistake of meeting her gaze. Her eyes gave her away. It was the expression that had gotten to him ever since she was a little girl.

"Are you warm enough now?"

She nodded and stood. "This side is definitely cooked to perfection."

"Then let's sit on the couch before I have to explain a one-sided tan to your mother."

She took the hand he offered, and the slight widening of her eyes told him that she felt the same spark he had. He led her to the sofa and they sat down. On the pretext of settling in, he moved so that no part of their bodies touched. A man could only stand so much.

"I've been thinking about something, Steve."

"What?" He braced himself for anything and she took so long to answer, he dreaded her response. What she said surprised him.

"I've been wondering how to extricate ourselves from this situation."

"'Situation'?" he said. "'Extricate'?"

He knew what she was talking about, but the question gave him a chance to throw some ice water on the anger bubbling inside him. How could she be so cool and clinical about this? He wasn't sure where the feeling came from, but knew he would be up to his neck in alligators if he explored it too thoroughly. Especially when she was so close, he could reach over and pull her into his arms.

"You know. This marriage." She wrapped her hands around her mug and stared into the fire just a few feet away. "We need to make some decisions. Like what to tell everyone when we split up."

There it was again: white-hot anger. He detoured from the flash point—her reference to separating. "We haven't discussed what to tell them about why we married in the first place."

She looked at him and her eyes were huge and haunted and so beautiful he could easily lose himself in them. "I've been thinking about it and this is what I decided our story should be. It happened very fast. We were there, it seemed right, we did it. All of that is true."

As far as it went, he thought. "Then what?"

"I'd appreciate it if you could stick around for a few weeks after the baby is born. Then I'll tell them it's not working for me. I thought I was in love with you. But I was wrong and we decided to end the marriage before destroying any chance of a friendship."

"What about the baby?"

"They'll have to know the truth. Otherwise they would believe you're the father and hold you responsible for something you didn't do. They would hate you. I'd never forgive myself for that."

He wasn't worried about Flo and Tom Marchetti. At least, not too much. Nick was another story. Since they were kids, Steve had always understood and abided by the hands-off-Rosie rule. And, except for the kiss, he'd followed the prime directive. He walked a fine line by marrying Nick's little sister. That kiss had him teetering dangerously. Now he felt as if he were working without a net.

"This is your gig. Tell them what you want," he finally said.

"I'll take all the blame, Steve. You've been so generous." She crossed her arms over her abdomen in an unconscious gesture to protect the baby growing there.

He felt the prick of guilt. Would she have been so

anxious to formulate an extrication plan if she'd married Wayne?

He knew he would hate her answer, but he couldn't help asking, "Do you miss the weasel?"

Her lips tightened, but he saw the gleam of mischief in her eyes. "I assume you mean Wayne?"

He just looked at her.

"I miss him dreadfully. My heart is broken and I don't think I'll ever recover. You've ruined my life, Steve, and I'll never forgive you."

"So you're fine with it."

"I hate that you know me so well." She moved closer and punched him playfully in the shoulder. Her thigh hugged his. She put her hand on his knee as she thought for a moment. "I never loved him."

"You sound sure about that."

"I am. I talked him into marrying me for the sake of the baby."

"Bet you didn't have to talk very long or hard," he said sarcastically.

"A lot you know about it," she countered. "Actually, it took some fast talking on my part to convince him. He said he loved me and didn't want to get married for the wrong reason. He didn't want to hurt me."

"But he took the money and ran."

"I think that had more to do with my family than with me. He didn't want to jeopardize my relationship with them."

"As opposed to staying and facing his responsibilities, which would prove to them that he was good enough for you."

"I already told you I didn't love him. Why are you on this mission to assassinate his character?"

"Because—" He looked at her. "I'm ticked that you waited so long to confirm my suspicion that you didn't love him and spare me more guilt."

He'd held his breath, praying she wouldn't pick up on the word *more* and grill him about it. It wasn't that he regretted breaking up her wedding. He felt guilty about checking out her former fiancé in the first place. No one had asked him to, and he still wasn't sure why he'd felt compelled to do it. The evidence he'd compiled convinced him that there was no way she could marry that creep. The word "lowlife" was too good for him. Steve resolved as soon as possible to get those pictures back from Mrs. M. and destroy them. Rosie would never see them. She never had to know what a despicable bastard the guy was.

"Guilt builds character," she said.

"I think I'm pretty heavy in the character department," he said smugly.

"Yes, you are," she answered, her tone suddenly serious. She put a protective hand over her abdomen again. "You married us and gave us your name. That will mean a lot when we're alone."

There it was, that look again. There was no time for rational thought. The action was instinctive. He pulled her into his lap and folded her into his arms.

"You'll never be alone," he said.

"I know." She snuggled closer. "But you did something for me that no one in my family could do." She leaned away and looked at him. "I'll always love you for it."

It was just an expression. He knew that. It was for what he'd done, not who he was, he knew that, too. But the words touched him in a place not even Rosie had been able to reach before.

He tunneled his fingers into her hair. His heart pounded as he stared into her eyes. His gaze traveled lower, to her full lips. Maybe if he'd never tasted her before, he would have been able to resist. But he *had* kissed her, and he wanted to again, more than he wanted his next breath.

He dipped his head and touched his mouth to hers. The shiver that rippled through her had nothing to do with cold. He knew that because when he looked, he saw passion in her eyes. That was something he understood. His blood warmed and raced through his veins, sending liquid heat to every part of his body.

He needed her. He wanted to make love with her.

There was a small distant voice whispering frantically in his ear that it was wrong. He listened for a moment, and pulled back slightly, staring into Rosie's flushed face and passion-dazed eyes. Her ragged breathing matched his own.

"Don't, Steve—"

His name was a plea on her lips, and he could no more deny her than he could resist the expression in her eyes that once again said loud and clear, "Don't leave me out."

She took his face in her hands and pulled his mouth to hers. He kissed her back, then trailed nibbling caresses over her cheek, down her neck, then back up to the soft, responsive spot just beneath her ear.

"Make love to me, Steve."

He blinked the passion haze from his eyes. "Are you sure?" he asked, his voice a ragged whisper.

"Yes," she said with complete conviction.

Steve stood with Rosie in his arms and carried her to the master bedroom where he set her on the bed. She slid over to make room for him, and sighed contentedly when he lowered himself beside her and gathered her close. He kissed her lips, her eyes, her cheeks, and the spot beneath her ear that he found was especially responsive.

He slipped his hand beneath her shirt and touched her breast, smiling at her moan of pleasure. He wished her life would only be filled with moments like that. As long as he could, he would do his best to see that nothing bad touched her.

Rosie wondered at the frown on Steve's face. Before she could ask, he moved his hand to her other breast, shooting pleasure through her like a rocket. She wished she knew what fairy godmother she should thank for making this dream come true. She finally felt married and the honeymoon was about to start.

She unbuttoned his shirt, and ran her hands over the muscled contours of his chest. Her palms tingled at the masculine covering of hair. His breathing grew more harsh and she reveled in her power. She'd wished once to shake him from his complacency. She'd finally done it and would give anything to know *how*.

Then he kissed her and everything else was forgotten. In a haze of pleasure and passion, Steve took her to a place she had never been before. It was a perfect world. He learned her body and its secrets until he'd taken her to the heights of desire. Then he buried himself inside her, and together they jumped into a dizzying spiral of release.

Tired beyond belief, Rosie was vaguely aware when Steve pulled her into his arms. He made her feel safe and secure. That was her last thought before sleep claimed her.

* * *

Rosie awoke to bright sunlight streaming through the crack in the curtains and Steve's arm thrown possessively across her waist. They were lying spoon fashion, his chest to her back. And neither chest nor back was clothed. For a moment she thought she must be dreaming. She pinched her arm and broke into a wide grin when she felt it and knew she was wide awake.

She had thought this would never happen. After finding a tall blonde in his apartment with him, she had resigned herself to life without Steve. She had made up her mind that she would find a man who could care about her the way she wanted. She would live happily ever after with him.

Last night changed everything.

Steve hadn't actually said he loved her. But didn't actions speak louder than words? Everything he had done for her, *to her,* convinced her that he had romantic feelings for her.

"A perfect world," she whispered.

Steve's arm tightened across her abdomen and nestled her more closely to his muscular length. His breath stirred her hair. Waking up in his arms was better than anything she'd ever imagined. She grinned from ear to ear.

Then he tensed. She had a bad feeling and her happy bubble started losing air.

"Oh, God," she heard him groan.

He removed his arm and rolled onto his back, away from her.

Rosie did the same, then turned her head to peek at him. He rubbed a hand over his face and she heard the rasp of whiskers against his palm.

"Don't say you're sorry," she said, trying to keep her tone light and teasing. *She* knew there was a desperate "please" at the beginning of that statement, but if God was merciful, Steve wouldn't guess.

"Okay. I won't say it." He didn't look at her but she saw that his hands were clenched. "It's just—"

"What?" she prompted. This was like taking a bullet and trying not to breathe because the pain would be excruciating. Just get it over with, she thought. "What?" she said again.

"This is all my fault." He glanced at her then. "I never meant for that to happen."

"But it did."

"Yeah."

"Now what?"

"I don't want you to get the wrong idea, Ro."

"What's the right one?" she asked.

"Things got out of hand. We got caught up in the moment. That's all."

She heard it again. That sound she'd heard when he'd pulled back from her in the woods. Her heart was cracking. She prayed for the strength to keep him from seeing.

"Of course that's all. What more would there be?" she asked with as much nonchalance as she could muster.

"Not a darn thing." He stared hard at her and she wondered what he was thinking.

"We're consenting adults. I'm an independent woman. For goodness' sake, it's practically expected. We're married." She couldn't ever remember talking being so painful. "When are you going to get that through your head? You're as bad as my parents, worrying about me. I'm a grown-up. Perspective is my middle name. Last night was—''

He put his finger to her lips. ''At ease. You convinced me. I'm glad you agree that it shouldn't happen again. Thanks for understanding, Ro. I'm going to take a shower.''

Understanding? Things were clear as mud, she thought.

She looked away as he rolled out of bed. Not because she was embarrassed to see him now. She was afraid he would see the tears that blurred her vision. Sitting up, she pressed her forehead to her knees. Would she ever again be able to draw a breath without pain? Willing herself to get the message, she chanted, ''He will never love me.''

As he closed the bathroom door, Steve heard Rosie mumble something. He turned the water on as hot as he could stand, then let it pound his head and shoulders. He hoped it would wash at least part of the sin from his soul. All these years he'd kept his distance from Rosie to prevent exactly this. He'd broken the cardinal rule. And that wasn't the worst of his crime. Now that he knew the sweetness of her, inside and out, it would be that much harder to keep his hands and his emotions to himself.

That would only compound his mistake. He'd been with women before; he believed women wanted him. But love? That wasn't in the cards for him. It never had been and never would be. He'd come to terms with that fact years ago. People who were supposed to love you ran out on you. About the same time he'd realized that, he found out something else about himself.

Never take the chance of needing anyone.

When the water turned cold, he shut it off and stepped out. After what he'd done, he couldn't stay alone with her even one more night. He would tell her he had to get back to town. Plead work.

Steve slipped on his jeans and stepped out of the bathroom drying his hair. He caught a glimpse of Rosie, wearing his shirt. With her dark hair falling wildly around her face and shoulders, she looked like a woman who had just been well satisfied by a man. He grew hard at the thought. He'd prepared himself for this but hadn't anticipated that it would happen so soon—or so powerfully.

Then her look of distress penetrated his foggy brain. "Nick's here," she said, sounding frantic. "He's here right now!"

"Nick? What's—" Then he remembered. With everything that had happened, the casually issued invitation had completely slipped his mind.

A movement in the doorway drew his attention. Nick Marchetti stood there for several seconds and it was impossible to mistake the rage vibrating through him. He moved slowly, stopping in front of Steve.

"You backstabbing son of a bitch."

Nick had always known he wasn't good enough for Rosie. Steve had finally proved him right.

Steve didn't see the punch coming and wouldn't have blocked it if he had. A second later pain exploded in his head.

Chapter Seven

Shocked to her core by the single act of violence, Rosie couldn't move for several moments. Then she positioned herself between the two men and stood her ground in spite of her trembling. She managed a glare for Nick that would have done her mother proud. If he made another move toward Steve, she would stop him.

"How dare you?" she asked. "What gives you the right to walk in here and hit Steve?"

Nick gave her a brief glance. "You're a Marchetti. That's all the reason I need." Then he turned his steely eyed look on Steve. "Mother sent you to stop her wedding, not sleep with her."

He took one step, and Rosie grabbed his arm, hanging on for all she was worth. "I'm a consenting adult and this is the nineties. What I do is none of your business."

"I'm making it my business." When her brother

yanked away, she stumbled and Steve caught her around the waist, steadying her.

"Watch it, Nick." His voice hummed with anger. "She's—"

"Not going to put up with the heavyweight championship of the world," Rosie said quickly. Steve had been about to spill the beans about her pregnancy. This was not the time or the place. Instead of a single punch, she would have World War III on her hands.

"Sorry, Rosie," Nick said. "It would be best if you leave us alone. I'll take care of him for you. Then we can go home."

She put her hands on her hips and frowned at him as her temper simmered. "If I needed your help, big brother, I would have asked for it."

"He's right, Ro. This is between him and me." Steve looked down at her. "Give us a few minutes alone to talk."

Some things never changed. They were leaving her out again. Only when they were children, Steve had almost always included her. She frowned at Nick. "You burst in here uninvited and—"

"I asked him to come," Steve said.

"What?" She looked up at him and noticed redness around his right eye. It was going to swell and needed ice, but she was afraid to leave these two baboons alone long enough to get it. Correction—one baboon and his punching bag. Steve hadn't lifted a finger to defend himself.

"I invited him up for the weekend," Steve said again. "It slipped my mind."

That wasn't a big surprise, considering everything that had happened. But everyone knew her brother was a notorious workaholic. He thrived on working weekends. Why had he chosen this one to take off? His timing needed serious fine tuning.

She looked at her brother. "You'd rather have a root canal than R and R. What are you doing here?"

"Mother was worried."

"Why?"

"She got a brief message from him." He nodded in Steve's direction. "That was almost two weeks ago. She's worried."

"Why didn't she just use the telephone?" Rosie asked.

"She tried and couldn't get through."

Rosie thought back over the last two weeks and tried to recall if they'd used the phone. She'd threatened to call a cab to go into town, but hadn't gotten farther than pulling out the directory. She walked into the living room, self-conscious that she wore nothing more than Steve's shirt. It came to just above her knees and was big on her, a very good thing. Signs of the pregnancy were becoming obvious and she knew how observant Nick was. In certain clothes, he wouldn't miss her rounded tummy.

She picked up the receiver and listened. There was no dial tone. Steve checked the wall and held up the other end of the cord that was not plugged into the jack. "Here's the problem," he said.

"Premeditated seduction." Nick scowled. "Didn't even want the phone to get in the way. Right, Schafer?"

"It's not like that," Rosie said. "Plugging in the phone was the last thing on our minds."

As soon as the words were out of her mouth Rosie wished to call them back. The dark look on Nick's face turned thunderous and his hands curled into fists.

"My own sister." He moved forward and Rosie stepped in his path. He stopped, but didn't look at her. Over her head he met Steve's gaze. "I never figured you for a low-down dirty creep."

Rosie felt Steve's hands on her arms as he tried to move her out of the way. She wasn't budging. He stepped around her and squarely faced her brother. "Nick, you don't know all the facts. Don't jump to conclusions—"

"I didn't jump to anything. You slept with my sister. She was on the rebound and you took advantage of her."

Rosie moved beside Steve in a show of unity. Nick's black eyes burned like coals, but she refused to look away.

Rosie was at a complete loss to understand why he was so angry. He'd been the most outspoken of her brothers about his dislike of Wayne. She'd expected him to be giddy with superiority that she'd found out what a jerk the guy was. She'd expected him to be pompous with approval that she'd wound up with his best friend. There was one small detail he needed to know that might make the difference in his approval.

"It's not taking advantage if you're married," she said.

"Married?" Stunned, Nick looked from one to the other.

She nodded. "Almost two weeks now."

The muscle in Nick's cheek contracted. He stared at her hard. "So he stopped your marriage to the weasel and snapped you up himself?"

"No one forced me to say the words," Rosie said, lifting her chin.

"What's wrong with you, Rosie?"

Steve stood beside her. "Don't blame her, Nick."

"We didn't send you to break up the wedding with Wayne so *you* could marry my sister. I thought we were friends."

"We are," Steve said.

"I don't understand how you could do this." Frustrated, Nick turned away for a moment, running a hand through his dark hair. When he turned back, the fury glittered brighter in his eyes. "You never said a word. You always swore that no woman would snag you. How could you do this?"

Rosie stared at her brother for several moments, letting his words sink in. Finally she said, "I don't think you give two hoots about me, Nick. You're upset that Steve didn't consult you." She put her hands on her hips. "I think you're more ticked off about losing your bachelor buddy than anything else."

"You are so far off base, Rosie."

"Am I?"

"Yeah. A buddy doesn't up and marry his best friend's sister without warning. I thought I knew you, Schafer. After all these years, and everything we've been through together, this is a hell of a way to find out that I don't know you at all."

The muscle in Steve's arm contracted as his hand curled into a fist. "Nick, listen to me—"

"There's nothing you can say that I want to hear." He looked at Rosie. "I'm leaving. Are you coming with me?"

She reached a hand toward him. "Nick, let's talk about this—"

"Are you coming or not?"

"No."

Without another word, he walked out the front door.

Rosie started to follow, but Steve stopped her with a hand on her shoulder. She turned to look up at him, but his image wavered from the moisture in her eyes. He folded her into his arms. "It'll be okay, Ro. Give him time to cool off."

Tears didn't blur her hearing. There was a whole range of emotion in his voice. Anger, frustration, regret. And most of all, sadness. She had never heard this voice from Steve before and it tore at her. This mess was all her fault. Surely there must be something she could do to set things right. Letting the wrong impression fester in Nick's mind longer than necessary didn't seem smart. She could fix the problem in thirty seconds. In fact, she didn't understand why Steve hadn't told him that he'd married her to protect her. Although Nick hadn't given them time to explain much of anything. But it wasn't too late. She could catch him.

She wriggled free of his hold. "Let's go after him, Steve. We'll tell him what's going on. He'll understand."

"And thank me?" The words oozed bitterness that she knew was self-directed.

"Yes."

"No. You're his baby sister and I crossed the line. He'll never understand. Marchettis don't forgive."

"That's not fair. I'm a Marchetti. I'm not too stubborn to admit when I'm wrong."

He released her, and gave her a wry look. "Yeah, like the way you came clean right away about not being in love with Wayne?"

"That was different—"

"It always is, Rosie."

She sighed and he gave her a half smile to match his half-closed right eye. It was the most endearing look and she felt the tug all the way to her heart. His poor face. His best friend had done that. What were they going to do? Lifting her hand, she gently touched the puffiness in his cheek. She pulled back when he winced. "Sorry. I'll get some ice for that."

"No." He shook his head. "Let's just get out of here."

His bleak tone, so unlike him, robbed her of the will to argue. As she packed her things, she couldn't forget the animosity she'd seen between the two men. The only good thing, if she could call it that, was that the ugly scene had taken her mind off Steve's morning-after-the-night-before rejection.

It was a one-time insanity. "Caught up in the moment," Steve had said. "Things got out of hand," he'd said. She had done her best to hide her pain, but it hurt that he could trivialize such a beautiful experience. It was something she had dreamed about for a long time. But she would give it up in a heartbeat if it would bring Steve and Nick back together again.

They had always been best friends. Although he'd never said it in so many words, Steve considered Nick the brother he'd never had. The only time she'd ever seen friction between the two was when Steve let her tag along over her brother's objections. This marriage was one humongous tagalong.

Nick had to know the truth about it, about how Steve had given her his last name to save her reputation. She would love to see her always-superior big brother with egg on his face. And she would make sure his apology to Steve was long, eloquent, and as humiliating as possible. More important, if she didn't do something soon, the rift might be irreparable.

When they were ready to leave, Steve loaded the luggage into the car. Before he opened the door for her, she said, "I've been thinking about something."

"What?"

"We have to go straight to my folks and break the news that we're married."

"By the time we get there it'll be old news."

"I know. But we have to tell them the *whole* truth, about why we got married, I mean."

He stared down at her and gave her a look that turned her heart over. It continued to pound and her breath caught in her throat when he took her face in his hands and kissed her on the forehead. "It's not the marriage Nick is so upset about, Ro."

"Oh." Her cheeks burned. "But we were married when that happened."

"That's probably why he only belted me once. But you're his little sister. Nothing else matters."

"That's silly. If he knows why you married me, he'll get over all of it."

"I don't think so. But let's cross one bridge at a time. Okay?"

"Whatever you say."

"Does that mean Miss Grown-up, Independent Woman is going to let me do the talking?" he asked with a slow half smile.

"Whatever you say," she repeated.

But when the time came, she wouldn't let him take any more heat from her family. She would explain how she'd gotten herself into this mess and how Steve had generously saved her rear end. It would be hard, telling them everything she'd done. But somehow the prospect of facing her parents, and getting The Look, wasn't as formidable with Steve by her side. When it was over, she knew she would have his support to pick up the pieces.

At least for now, she thought sadly.

Steve and Rosie walked up the steps to the Marchetti house. It was a big, sprawling place with manicured lawns in the front and pool with brick-trimmed patio in the rear. It was the kind of home Steve had always yearned for but knew he would never have. A condo was sufficient for a bachelor. Technically he wasn't one anymore, but he would be. The sooner the better. Rosie was a temptation that he couldn't afford. Sleeping with her had only made it worse. Sleeping with her again would compound the mistake.

Steve wasn't looking forward to facing Flo and Tom Marchetti with the news that he'd married their daughter. No matter that the duration of the union would be as short as he could make it, he was the last man they would have chosen for her. Nick's furious reaction had confirmed that suspicion.

He glanced behind him at the circular drive and the four cars lined up in front of his. "I see the forces are mobilized."

"Looks that way," Rosie snapped, her voice tight with nerves.

All her brothers were here. Steve figured that was a good news, bad news situation. He only had to do this once. The bad news—Alex and Joe had tempers equal to or greater than Nick's. Luke was different. Even his looks weren't vintage Marchetti. The others all had dark eyes and nearly black hair. Luke's eyes were blue, his hair lighter brown. The youngest Marchetti male let his anger simmer and gather strength. But when the storm broke, watch out. This time, it would be four against one.

Rosie met his gaze and said, "I'll protect you."

Make that four against two. "Don't shoot until you see the whites of their eyes."

He smiled, thinking about little Rosie trying to protect him from Nick. Five feet and a bit against six feet two inches of wiry strength, and she'd never flinched. She'd known Nick wouldn't hurt her physically. But that might have been easier to bear than his disapproval. Her family was very important to her. He just hoped this charade to give her and the baby his name for protection didn't cost her the people she cared about. Steve knew he could deal with it. He'd never known any different. But Rosie had.

She took a deep breath. "Ready?" she asked.

"Damn the torpedoes, full speed ahead."

"War terms are so comforting," she said with a sigh as she lifted the brass door knocker and let it fall.

Almost instantly, Flo Marchetti answered. Steve always noticed what a handsome woman she was. Taller than her daughter, Mrs. M. wore her dark hair in a short, sophisticated style. Her off-white pants and matching hip-length top suited her figure. She smiled at her daughter and opened her arms. Rosie went to her without hesitation.

"I missed you, Ma," Rosie said, a catch in her voice.

"Not enough to call," the older woman answered, and winked at Steve. "The least you could have done was tell us the good news."

"Good news?" Rosie asked hesitantly. She

stepped out of her mother's embrace. "Nick told you that Steve and I are married. That good news?"

"That's it. You have some explaining to do." She looked at Steve. "But first, how about a hug from my new son?"

That surprised him, shocked him right down to his socks. A hug wasn't even close to taking shots at him, with torpedoes or anything else. She was probably saving that for Mr. M. Steve moved forward and reluctantly accepted her show of affection. One down, five to go.

The older woman stood between them and linked her arms through theirs to walk the length of the entryway. "Rosemarie, this is so romantic. Just like one of those novels you love so much in your store. Come inside, you two, and tell us everything. The whole clan is here."

"How come, Ma?" Rosie asked.

"Because I called them. I knew you would stop here. Now, go in the family room. I have things to do in the kitchen." She looked sympathetically at Steve. "You need some ice on that eye, dear."

Steve nodded as he took Rosie's coat and hung it with his in the hall closet. Then they walked into the comfortable family room. There was a blaze in the brick fireplace on the far wall. A burgundy leather sofa and love seat rested perpendicular to it. Expensive oak furniture was tastefully arranged on plush champagne-colored carpet. The Marchetti men were also arranged, standing shoulder to shoulder, front and center, in descending order of age and rank. There were those military analogies again, he thought ruefully.

Mr. M., tall and gray-haired, Nick the image of his

father. Joe, the same height as the other two, but more muscular. Alex, the same height and wearing wire-rimmed glasses, then Luke, who was about two inches shorter. The three oldest brothers had Marchetti written all over them. Luke had caught some dormant genes somewhere along the line, but he was no less tough-looking than his brothers.

Tom Marchetti smiled. "You two look like you're facing a firing squad."

Steve glanced at Rosie and saw her wince at the words. She took a deep breath. "Dad, I have something—"

"I'll do this. Remember?" Steve gave her a reassuring grin as he took her hand and gently squeezed. Then he turned back to the five men and concentrated his attention on her father. "Sir, I have something to tell you."

"Shoot. And make it quick," the older man said. "You need some ice for that shiner."

"I married Rosie two weeks ago." That was as quick as he could make it.

Steve resisted the urge to duck. One by one, he looked her brothers straight in the eye. He could tell that Nick was still furious, but he had no clue as to what the rest were thinking. Rosie was easy to read. When Steve met her gaze, he saw apprehension.

Tom Marchetti cleared his throat and finally spoke, breaking the tension. "Why didn't you tell us? We would have liked to have been there for our only daughter's wedding."

Steve didn't regret taking charge of the talking. Not much anyway. "It all happened so fast we didn't have time."

Flo Marchetti brought in a tray with fluted glasses

filled with a bubbly golden liquid. "Isn't this wonderful news, everyone?"

Steve braced himself, waiting for the explosion. It came, but not at all what he expected. Four out of five Marchetti men broke into smiles and hugged Rosie, then clapped him on the back, shaking his hand to congratulate him. Then Mrs. M. passed out the champagne. Everyone but Nick took a glass.

"I want to know what his angle is," he said angrily.

Mrs. M. held out the remaining flute, until he finally curled his fingers around it. "I already know," she said.

Steve looked at Rosie. Her eyes were wide and puzzled, with a dash of apprehension thrown in. She lifted her shoulders slightly as if to say she hadn't a clue what her mother knew.

Flo looked at the men in her family. "It was just a matter of time until Rosie and Steve got together. These two have been sweet on each other since they were children."

"Mother—" Rosie's cheeks turned a becoming pink.

"Don't 'mother' me. I was there. You hounded me for contacts and a makeover for your sixteenth birthday party because Steve agreed to be your date."

Rosie moved beside her mother and put her arm around the taller woman. "Ma, no one wants to remember this. Especially me."

Steve didn't know whether to duck or run when Alex walked over to him. Then he noticed a twinkle in the other man's eyes. "I want to hear more. What about you, bro?" he asked, looking at Steve.

Did he only imagine it, or did Alex's affectionate "bro" have more significance than usual?

Rosie glared at her brother. "No one cares about it, Alex. That's ancient history."

"Yeah, that's why you married the guy." Her brother winked.

Hearing the confirmation of her crush pleased him—probably more than it should. He recalled that it was right around her sixteenth birthday when Nick had made it clear that his little sister was off limits. Because of that, Steve had stood her up, putting the kibosh on her crush. Just in time.

His first glimpse of her without glasses, wearing makeup and a new hairstyle was branded into his memory. She'd become a woman practically before his eyes; he'd found her irresistible. Spending time with her was out of the question if he had any hope of complying with the hands-off-Rosie-rule. Guilt stabbed him again as he remembered how good she'd felt in his arms. Which just confirmed that he didn't belong. A guy good enough for her would have understood and obeyed the rule.

Steve felt less like a brother-in-law and more like an outlaw. But he said to Alex, "I think we should let Rosie off the hook."

Mr. M. nodded once, emphatically. "My little girl is in good hands." Then he held up his champagne glass. "I propose a toast to my daughter and the man I always considered my son. It's official now. Welcome to the family, Steve. Let's drink to Mr. and Mrs. Steve Schafer."

A chorus of cheers went up before all but one of the group clinked glasses and sipped. Steve watched Rosie put the glass to her lips. He glanced around, certain no one else noticed that she just pretended to drink, reminding him of secret number two.

He was having serious second thoughts about his sweeping declaration to do the talking. He knew Rosie wanted to tell her family about the baby. It was a mystery to him why, but the majority of Marchettis seemed to be genuinely happy about the marriage. He was reluctant to tell them the rest and put a damper on this celebration.

Nick forcefully set his untouched champagne on the oak table beside him. He put the fingers of one hand to the palm of the other, forming a T. "Time out. Just like that, you all accept this marriage? Doesn't anyone else want to know why it happened so fast?" Nick looked around. "He went to stop Rosie from marrying the creep, then she comes home his bride. Am I the only one who thinks that's weird?"

Again Rosie started to say something, but Steve jumped in before she could respond. "It *was* fast. We're sorry about that. But we were there with the justice of the peace and we knew that's what we wanted to do. It's as simple as that."

Nick furiously shook his head. "I don't buy it. He's the only guy I know as set against marriage as me."

"What about me?" Alex asked.

"Better Steve than me," Joe chimed in. "It'll be a cold day in hell before a woman gets me to the altar. What about you, Luke?"

The youngest Marchetti shrugged noncommittally. "It's not tops on my list of Must Do's."

"Spoken like an accountant," Joe said. "Come on, Luke—"

"Leave him alone," Flo interrupted. Then she

looked at Nick. "You're the oldest. You set the example. I've never understood your antipathy to marriage, Nicholas. I wish you would explain."

"Marriage sucks you dry and leaves nothing."

Mrs. M. looked like she'd gotten more than she bargained for, although she covered it well. "That's certainly cynical. And exactly how would you know that? You've never been married."

He stuck his hands in his pockets. "I've seen it happen," he said.

"What have you seen, Nick?" Tom asked, sounding concerned.

"It's all about what a woman can get from a man."

Rosie made a small noise and Steve glanced at her. The blood had drained from her face. She took Nick's words personally, as a judgment of her. Steve moved to her side and casually slipped his arm around her waist. He had no idea why Nick felt this way, but his and Rosie's situation wasn't like that. She didn't want anything from him. In fact, he'd had to do some fast talking to convince her to marry him. Getting her through this with minimal battle damage was important to him.

Mrs. M. sipped her drink. "I don't know what couples you've seen who are so dysfunctional, Nick, but not every marriage is like that. This is your sister's celebration. Don't spoil it." She shot him a warning look, then said, "I'm going to get Steve some ice for his eye. Would you like some for your hand?"

Together Steve and Nick said, "I don't need any."

Instead of laughing at their habit of saying the same thing simultaneously, Nick glared. Then he met his mother's gaze. "All right, Mom. I won't spoil Rosie's night."

He turned on his heel and walked out. That was the second time in one day he'd done that.

"Nick—" Rosie ran after him, but the front door slammed before she could get there. She'd always had a special bond with Nick. He was the oldest, she was the baby. Steve hated this split between them. For the time being, there wasn't anything he could do to repair it. The success of their plan depended on everyone believing they were a couple.

After several seconds Tom Marchetti walked over to his daughter and pulled her into a hug. "Nick never did like surprises. And he got used to bossing you around. Don't worry, honey. He'll get over it. A day or two and he'll be happier for you than we are."

"Your father's right," Flo said. "We need to arrange a church ceremony and reception. After all, a justice of the peace—" She stopped and shook her head disapprovingly.

"No, Ma," Rosie interrupted. "There's something—" She hesitated.

"What is it, honey?" her father asked. "This is a happy occasion. Why shouldn't we gather our friends and family for a public celebration of your marriage? Give me one good reason."

Steve looked at Rosie, her hands intertwined and resting protectively over her abdomen. That was why.

This was his chance to tell them about the baby. Steve wondered if that news and the real reason for the wedding would repair the damage to his relationship with Nick. He looked around. To his surprise, everyone else was not only approving, but excited for them. He didn't understand it; he couldn't trust it. But he found his protective instincts for Rosie spilling over to include her family. Could he spoil their elation with that kind of announcement? Should he? They would have to know soon; Rosie was already starting to show. But did it have to be tonight?

Beside him, Steve felt Rosie bracing herself to announce her pregnancy. Something told him to stop her. He couldn't take this happy moment away from her and her family.

Steve cleared his throat. "We appreciate the offer. But we want a chance to be alone before we share this news with anyone else."

Chapter Eight

It was nearly midnight when they managed to pull themselves away from her family's celebration. After all the nudging and winking and earthy comments about newly married couples needing time alone, Steve drove her home. He carried her suitcases through her bookstore and up the stairs to the apartment above. Rosie unlocked the door and he followed her inside. After some difficulty maneuvering the luggage in the small hallway, she turned on the lights and he looked around.

"This is nice," he said.

Surprised, Rosie glanced up from the stack of mail in her hand. "You've seen it before," she said.

"Nope. Never."

She thought back over the last couple years since she'd moved in and opened the store. She couldn't remember him ever stopping by. Looking at him now, his large, very attractive frame filling her small apartment, she knew that if he had been here, she would never have been able to forget the image. Which is probably why she'd never invited him. It seemed like she'd been trying to put Steve out of her mind her whole life and she'd finally found a place that had no memories of him.

She shrugged. "Sorry. I didn't realize."

She looked around, feeling as though she'd been gone for a couple of years instead of only a few weeks. So much had happened. They were married, if you could call it that. Her family had taken the news better than she had dared hope, which was bittersweet. She couldn't help wishing that Steve *did* have romantic feelings for her as they thought. And though it didn't matter because Mr. and Mrs. Schafer wouldn't be sharing living quarters, she couldn't help wondering how "her husband" would like the rest of her place.

He punched the switch beside him and illuminated the dining area. The chandelier's gold and crystal sparkled, highlighting his face and the grooves beside his nose and mouth that always deepened when he was tired. The swelling from his shiner had gone down; now it was just a vivid shade of purple. Her hero. He tugged at her heart. Although she was his wife, she didn't feel she had the right to fuss over him. The situation stunk like the fine kettle of fish it was.

He glanced up at the delicate lamp hanging over the antique dining table Grandma Marchetti had given her. "Nice light," he said.

"'Nice light'?" she repeated, incredulous. "It's my pride and joy. That's like calling the Mona Lisa a nice wall hanging. Do you have any idea how long it took me to pay off that 'nice light'?"

"Sorry. Interior decorating isn't my area of expertise."

"Yeah, I guess if you knew Limoges from plastic it wouldn't do your image a whole lot of good." He was going to hate the rest of the place. But she offered anyway. "Would you like the tour? I know you're tired, but it'll only take about a second and a half."

"Sure."

"This is the living room," she said, lifting her arm in a sweeping gesture toward the small space. "The white love seats are my token insurrection."

"Against?"

"The meddling Marchettis. My mother told me the fabric would show every spot, so I bought them."

"And?" he prompted.

"She was right."

Rosie lead the way down the narrow hall toward the other half of her place. She pointed out the bathroom and continued on to her bedroom, the largest room. After flipping on the light she said, "Well? Take your best shot."

Her king-size four poster, matching oak dresser and armoire were big pieces of furniture, but she knew that's not what snagged his attention. He stared at the walls. "They're very pink."

"I grew up in a male-dominated household. It was my first chance to have the color I wanted without fear of being ridiculed. It's a girly color and I'm a girl."

"I've noticed."

As surely as an uneven sidewalk made her stumble, the two simple words tripped up her heart. It would be so easy to fall on her face. Covertly, she studied him. His expression gave no clue to what he was thinking—about her. She couldn't say the same about her choice of paint color. He loathed and despised rose parfait.

"I like this particular shade," she said defensively. "It's serene."

"Did I say anything?"

She pointed at him. "You were thinking it. Just as well. There's nothing you could say that my brothers haven't already." She turned off the light and he followed her out.

Passing the bathroom, Steve flipped on the light and caught her arm. "Whoa, Ro. Can we talk about this wallpaper?"

His shoulders seemed to span the doorway and she stood on tiptoe to see past him. He was still wearing his battered brown jacket and the faint smell of leather drifted to her along with the scent of his cologne. It was a heady combination with enough one-two punch to stagger her senses.

"You hate it, don't you?" she asked a little breathlessly as she met his gaze. "It's another mutiny moment. Ma said it was too bold."

Squinting, he held up his hand, pretending to shield his eyes from the glare. "Gold foil and paisley? I'd call it defiant and daring."

"You hate it," she said again.

"I didn't say that."

"You didn't have to."

"If anyone puts me on the spot, I'll deny this, but I think I might actually like it. The whole place. Somehow it all comes together. It's you—rebellious, independent, courageous and impertinent."

"If you say perky, I swear I'll black your other

eye.'' He laughed as she turned off the light and followed her into the kitchen. ''Want some tea?''

''Sure.''

''After tonight I don't feel especially courageous.''

''Why not?'' he asked, leaning a shoulder against the dining room wall while she bustled around.

''The folks still don't know about the baby. Every time I was going to jump in and say something, you changed the subject. Why?''

''It just didn't feel like the right time to tell them.''

''I thought maybe you were afraid that I would let them think you were the baby's father.''

He straightened abruptly and looked so startled it was almost funny. ''That never crossed my mind,'' he said.

She believed him. ''After the way they took the news about the wedding, if you were—junior's father, I mean—telling them would be a snap.''

''Yeah, they seemed happy.'' His words were low key, but his eyes told her he was bewildered by the reaction.

''Happy? Lottery winners aren't that happy. It would have been a good time to drop the bombshell.''

''I was more concerned about not spoiling their evening. They'll have to know soon, though.'' He glanced at her abdomen.

''It was very sweet of you to be so concerned about their feelings. But you're right. Soon everyone will see for themselves. Right now I just look like I'm putting on weight.'' She placed her hands over her abdomen.

As if the child within knew he was being discussed, there was a small movement. She froze, wanting to feel the wondrous sensation again. The baby had been moving around for a while now. At first she'd thought it was bubbles. Now she knew it was her child, and couldn't get enough of the miraculous feeling.

"Something wrong? What is it, Ro?"

She shook her head. "Something's very right. The baby's moving." She walked over to him and took his hand, placing it where she'd felt the activity. "Feel."

"Isn't it too early?" He tensed, but didn't try to pull away.

"The doctor says I could be farther along than he first thought. We won't know for sure until the ultrasound."

Then there was another motion and she knew by the awed expression on his face that Steve had felt it, too. "Wow," he said. "There's really something in there."

"Yeah," she said. "And when this something keeps getting bigger, the folks are going to ask questions. They need to know the truth." Then she had an "aha" experience. "Gotcha."

"What?"

"Tonight with my folks. You didn't say anything about the baby because you didn't want to see The Look, did you?"

"'The Look'?" He removed his hand from her tummy and stuck his fingertips into the pockets of his jeans.

She missed the warmth of his touch, the closeness and sharing they'd had for just an instant. Sadness stole over her and she tried to shake it off with a stern reminder to stop wishing for the moon. He was kind enough to be here at all. She could be alone through this. If not for his generosity, she would have no one to share the baby's progress, not to mention his last name.

"Yeah. When they know this marriage is just temporary, they'll be disappointed. Hence, The Look."

"What did your mother mean when she said it was only a matter of time until we got together?" he asked.

She didn't want to go where that question would lead because rejection and humiliation would surely follow. "That was Mama Marchetti matchmaking. Don't pay any attention."

She kept mental fingers crossed that her tone had been light enough, her expression casual enough, and above all, her hammering heart quiet enough to keep him from guessing there was anything more. The whistling teakettle made her jump. Quickly she grabbed it, then poured steaming water into the mugs she'd set out.

As she handed him one she said, "It's chamomile. Supposed to help you sleep. You look like you could use a good night's rest."

He nodded. "Yeah. So I think I'll move my things over in the morning."

Startled, Rosie jumped and spilled hot liquid on her wrist. Steve set his cup on the dining table and quickly moved beside her, leading her to the faucet where he let cold water soothe the minor irritation. His concern would have felt lovely except she was too stunned by what he'd said.

"Excuse me? You're moving in? Here?"

"Yeah."

"I don't recall inviting you."

He stared at her as if he'd been expecting this reaction and was ready for it. "We have to live some-where."

"Yes. You have your place and I have mine."

"Married people usually cohabitate."

"It's true. They do," she said, cautiously hopeful that he *wanted* to live with her. Maybe he cared for her more than he let on. "But my parents will know the truth soon enough so we don't have to keep up any pretense for them."

"This is a small town. People will talk."

"Okay." He really was concerned about her. Her heart beat a little faster. "But I think we should dis-cuss this."

"What's there to talk about?" he asked.

"For one thing, your place is bigger. The sleeping arrangements—"

"The couch here will be fine," he quickly inter-rupted.

The glow he'd kindled moments before began to flicker like a candle flame in a cold wind. "It's not very big or very comfortable."

"I'll manage."

"But why, Steve? Your place has four bedrooms; at least two of them don't have gym equipment in them. Why stay here and be uncomfortable?"

"One very practical reason. After the baby is born and we go back to the way things were, you won't have to move. With the new baby and all."

She held herself very still, hoping to keep the pain at bay. Even though she knew all the practical reasons for his marriage proposal, in a small corner of her heart she'd hoped it was simply that he cared for her. He was being very considerate. So why did it hurt so much when his practical, reasonable, sane, *unromantic* side reared its ugly head?

She took cover from the pain by diving right into her anger. She wasn't sure whether to kick him or grab a hunk of his sexy chest hair and yank for all she was worth. When would she learn to look at the world clearly instead of through the stars in her eyes? He was planning ahead because he couldn't wait for this inconvenient, unfortunate interlude to end.

"Look, I'll manage," she snapped. After taking a couple deep, cleansing breaths to check her temper, she continued. "I'll stay here, you go to your place and sleep in a bed where your feet won't hang off the end."

"If we don't make this look like a real marriage for a decent length of time, it could come back to bite you in the butt."

"How?"

He sighed. "We started this in the first place to avoid gossip. What about your folks and all their friends with grandchildren?"

"I'm beginning to not care very much what anyone thinks of me," she said.

"You're just tired, Ro. Why don't you get some sleep? In the morning—"

"This is my place. Don't you dare pat me on the head and send me to bed."

"That's not what I'm doing—"

"The heck it's not. Quit treating me like a little girl. I'm a grown woman. Hear me roar. I can take care of myself. You don't need to protect me."

"What about the baby?"

That brought her little tantrum to a screeching halt. He made her feel like the world's most self-centered woman. This child already wouldn't have an ideal world when he was born. How much worse would it be if people suspected the truth? She didn't want to raise her baby without a name. Steve was offering his.

"I'm sorry. You can stay. And Steve?" She wrapped her arms around his waist and rested her cheek on his chest.

"What?" His voice cracked.

"Thank you."

He tightened his hold momentarily. "My pleasure."

Six weeks later Steve felt like pond scum because they still hadn't told her parents about the baby. Mr. and Mrs. M. had been called to Grandma Marchetti's when she fell and broke her hip. Besides nursing her, then moving her into their home, business matters had kept his in-laws busy. They had been in touch by phone, but that wasn't how he and Rosie wanted to break the news. Circumstances had conspired to put it off, but that was going to change tonight.

Rosie had invited her parents to dinner so they could tell them in person.

One look at her person and they would know anyway. She was glowing with health and wearing maternity clothes to accommodate her blossoming figure.

He stirred the marinara sauce as instructed before she'd gone into her bedroom to get ready. She was nervous, wanted to look her best. As far as he was concerned, first thing in the morning, right after rolling out of bed, she looked pretty good to him. If he had known how hard it would be to see her every day, under such intimate circumstances, he probably would have taken a chance on separate habitation.

He slept on an air mattress in the living room. In all this time, he'd never set foot in the bedroom, not while Rosie was in it. But that didn't mean he could ignore her. Her crossword puzzle lay half finished on the table. Sneakers from her nightly walk rested by the front door. Most dangerous of all was the lingering fragrance of her perfume that made him think of her even when she wasn't there. These little things, and so many more conspired to never give him a moment's peace from wanting her.

His body reacted to that thought as usual—instantly and painfully. Footsteps on the stairs told him the Marchettis had used the key Rosie had given them.

"They're here, Ro." He heard a crash from the bedroom. "You okay?"

"There's no blood if that's what you mean." She hurried down the hallway. "But the short answer is no. I'm nervous as a long-tailed cat in a roomful of rocking chairs."

She wore a full-cut, black and white vertical-striped top and dressy black slacks. Her hair was secured on top of her head with the curls cascading down. He knew she'd spent a lot of time on her makeup, but he didn't think she needed any. She always looked beautiful.

"Wow," he said, letting his gaze travel over her from head to toe.

One of her dark brows shot up. "Your nose is growing, Schafer."

"Why would I lie?"

"Because you know your survival depends on it."

Before he could debate that further, there was a knock on the door. She looked at him sternly. "Do not say damn the torpedoes, or anything about shooting the whites of their eyes.''

"How about we're low on ammunition, make every shot count?''

She laughed and he thought her tension eased momentarily. Then she opened the door and he didn't mistake the stiff set of her shoulders, her trembling hand.

"Hi, Ma, Daddy,'' she said as the older couple stepped past her and into the living room. "How's Grandma?'' she asked, closing the door.

Her mother took off her coat and hung it on the rack in the corner. "She's fine. Luke said he'd stay with her tonight. Those two always had a special bond.'' She turned and stopped short as she gave her daughter a really good, head-to-toe once-over.

This was the first time Steve could remember seeing Flo Marchetti speechless. He moved to stand beside Rosie and they faced her parents side by side.

Her father cleared his throat. "My guess is that this is what you had to tell us.''

Rosie's hands twisted nervously. "I'm sorry I didn't tell you sooner. It's just that, Grandma got sick. You were busy. I didn't—'' She reached out in a helpless gesture.

Flo Marchetti's eyes filled with tears. "So this was the angle. Nicky was right.''

"Of course he was,'' Tom said, patting Rosie's gently rounded stomach.

"Yeah, this is the angle,'' Rosie said ruefully.

Her dad put his arm around her shoulders and hugged her to him. "Just now when I first saw you, so pregnant, I thought maybe Wayne was the father.

I was ready to find that two-bit son of a biscuit eater and beat the living daylights out of him.''

Steve looked in the man's black eyes and didn't question that he meant every single word. In that instant he knew where the Marchetti men had gotten their tempers. If Wayne was here, he would be up to his eyeballs in alligators. Ditto if any of Rosie's brothers decided to look for him.

Tom met his gaze squarely. ''This explains why you got married so suddenly without saying anything. You're going to be a father.''

Rosie shook her head. ''No, Daddy.'' Helplessly she looked at her mother. ''Ma. It's not what you think—''

The other woman stared lovingly at her daughter and touched her abdomen. ''I'm going to be a grandmother. That's what I think.''

''Yes, but...'' Rosie glanced at Steve and her dark eyes begged him to explain. ''Feel free to jump in anytime.''

Flo looked from one to the other and shook her finger at Rosie, pretending displeasure. ''I thought we shared everything, but you never said a word about you and Steve. I've always had my suspicions about you two, but I had no idea that you'd gotten together.''

'' 'Gotten together'?'' Rosie asked.

''You know, the wild thing,'' Mrs. M. answered.

''Mother!''

''You think I don't keep up? I know all the slang—the horizontal—''

''Ma, we get your drift.'' Rosie again looked to Steve for help with the explanation. ''Tell them what happened.''

One look at the murderous anger in Tom Marchetti's eyes had convinced Steve that the whole truth was a mistake. Rosie had accused him of protecting her family, and in this case she couldn't be more right.

Flo took her daughter's face in her hands. "Sweetheart, I know about the birds and the bees. What you two did is pretty obvious."

"Ma, you've got it all wrong."

"Oh, I understand." Mrs. M. winked. "You think we'll be upset that you and Steve didn't wait until you were married. We're not from the Stone Age, dear." She waved her hand in a dismissive gesture. "If it makes you feel any better, Nick wasn't conceived in the cabin on our honeymoon the way we always said."

Rosie's cheeks turned red as she covered her ears. "Not another word, Ma."

"Thirty-five years later I'm not ashamed to say that I was carrying him when your father and I took our vows."

Steve put his arms around Rosie when she buried her face against his chest. "I don't want to hear this," she said, her voice muffled.

Mrs. M. smiled at her husband. "This younger generation. They think they're so hip. Rosie, you have my permission to share this with your brothers, but I'm not sure they can handle it."

Steve didn't know how her brothers would take her parents' revelation, but figured all the Marchetti sons were less likely to do something stupid and get in trouble if they believed he'd fathered her baby. There would be no need to defend their little sister's honor until he and Rosie split up. The thought made him feel empty inside. Pushing away the sensation, he reminded himself that letting her go was best for her. She could find the right man, someone who knew what love and commitment were all about. He also knew he would lose the only family he'd ever known.

But there was no doubt in his mind that this was the right thing to do—for all of them.

With his arm around Rosie, he looked at the elder Marchettis. He forced a broad grin. "So, I guess you're not upset that Rosie and I are going to have a baby."

Chapter Nine

Rosie tiptoed down the hall, past the living room where Steve slept, and turned the corner into the kitchen. She turned on the dim, under-the-cupboard lights, hoping Steve wouldn't be disturbed. Although it would serve him right for insisting on moving in here when his place would have been more comfortable. Her next thought was that there wasn't a place in hell low enough for her.

She was hypercritical of the man who had let her parents believe he was the father of her baby!

She still couldn't take it in. Glancing at the microwave clock, she read 3:30 a.m. Her mind had whirled ever since her parents left. She hadn't slept a wink. Chamomile tea, that's the ticket, she thought.

As quietly as possible, she put water in the teakettle. After assembling cup and teabag, she watched and waited to grab the kettle before it whistled and woke Steve.

"No need to be quiet."

His deep voice from the doorway scared her sense-less. As she whirled around, the cup flew out of her hand and shattered on the tile floor. Heart pounding, she stared at him. "There must be a law against sneaking up on someone like that."

"I just wanted you to know I wasn't asleep and you were doing a lousy job of trying to keep the noise down anyway."

The teakettle whistled and she turned toward it. Before she could take a step, Steve stopped her. "There's broken glass. Your feet are bare."

Without another word, he lifted her into his arms and took her out of the kitchen. Her heartbeat, just slowing to normal after the start he'd given her, cranked back up again for a completely different rea-son. His sleeping attire was nothing but sweatpants, which left his chest bare. With her arms around his neck for balance, she felt the ripple of muscles in his shoulders and back.

She was exquisitely conscious of the fact that she wasn't wearing a robe over her floor-length, fleece nightgown. Only flesh-to-flesh contact could have been more intimate. Her skin grew hot and flushed and she suddenly felt as if she couldn't get enough air into her lungs. Her gaze locked with his and she saw a darkly intense look that thrilled her to her core. It was the same expression he'd worn in the cabin the night they'd made love. The most wonderful night of her life. She ached to be with him again.

He carried her into the dining room and hesitated. Around the corner, just a few feet away down the hall was her room. She wanted him to take her into her bed and lay down beside her. She yearned for his arms around her. Just a few more steps and they could be there. He cast a look in that direction and she felt him shiver.

Then he swallowed once and bent to set her on the dining room rug. As he did, her hand slipped down his chest, in a sort of caress, and she heard his small intake of breath. Her first thought was that he wanted her, and exhilaration raced through her. Then she got real and faced facts. It wasn't a reaction to her closeness, merely the exertion of lifting, and quite handily at that, a pregnant woman.

He quickly removed the screeching teakettle and grabbed the broom to sweep up the glass. As he worked, muscles rippled across his broad back. From her vantage point she decided the view was as impressive as his show of strength.

"Way to go, Schafer." Keep your voice light, she cautioned. "How's your back? Pull any of those chick-magnet muscles?"

Dumping the shards into the trash, he glanced at her over his shoulder. "You're as light as a feather, squirt. I know better than to get sucked into *that* conversation."

"Then how about this one?" She watched him replace the broom. "Why did you let my parents believe that you fathered my baby?"

When he looked at her, his face was momentarily unshuttered. She glimpsed raw emotion. She recognized the abandoned boy he'd been the first time she'd met him. She saw deep loneliness. Most of all, she felt as if she could reach out and touch his pain. Without another thought except to comfort, she crossed the short distance between them and put her arms around him.

He only hesitated a moment before folding her to

his hard length. "Why, indeed," he breathed against her hair.

"That's not an answer."

"I know. But it's the best one I've got."

"Sell it somewhere else, Schafer. I'm not buying that. If there's anyone who knows exactly what he's doing at all times, it's you."

Case in point: resisting the urge to take her into the bedroom. She would have gone in a second. But she knew firsthand that he had more self-control than a gymnastics team at an all-you-can-eat buffet.

He loosened the circle of his arms and leaned back to look at her. One eyebrow raised questioningly. "You couldn't be more wrong."

She could be and she had been. Case in point: agreeing to his proposal and their marriage. It had started out as a way to protect her reputation, no strings attached. But every time she turned around, he changed the rules, did something so unbearably sweet that she was in great danger of having her heart shattered as surely as the cup she'd just broken.

She was exhausted and couldn't sleep. Thoughts kept tumbling through her mind. He was willing to assume responsibility for her child! The nobility of that gesture brought tears to her eyes. She blinked them away. As unselfish as his gesture was, it complicated everything.

"We can stand here all night if you want, but I need some answers."

"Give me the questions."

"What name goes on the birth certificate? Are you going to lie forever? If so, how can we divorce without the Marchetti brothers looking for the nearest tar pit and feather pillow?'' She bit her lip for a moment to still the quivering. ''What made you do it?''

He folded his arms across his chest and she resisted the urge to sigh at the terribly masculine picture he presented. He was lost in thought for several moments before he finally said, ''Actually it was your father.''

''Daddy? He forced you? When?'' Her mind skipped back over the events of the evening. She would bet her favorite ''keeper'' book that his decision had been spontaneous.

''No force. It was his look when he mentioned Wayne.''

''What look? I didn't see anything.''

''You did, but wouldn't know how to interpret it.''

''So this is a guy thing?''

He grinned. ''Definitely a macho he-man moment.''

She glanced at the clock. ''It's almost four o'clock. You might want to interpret for me sometime soon so we can get some sleep.''

''It's not complicated. You and I both know the Marchetti temper is a well-documented phenomenon. You're the one who mentioned tar and feathers in the same sentence with the Marchetti brothers.'' When she nodded her concurrence, he continued. ''Tonight I saw where they got it. If your family believed that Wayne the Weasel fathered your baby and skipped out on you, they would hunt him down and make him pay.''

''You're being overly dramatic.''

''Maybe. Are you willing to take that chance?'' He stared at her, and the silence grew. ''I'm not,'' he assured her, deadly serious.

''But, Steve—''

He shook his head. "Trust me on this, Ro. If any of your brothers decided to avenge your honor, someone could wind up in deep water with a leaky rowboat."

She had no workable knowledge of the male thought process. If Steve was right and she came clean with her family, one or all of her brothers could wind up in trouble. She would never forgive herself for that. As much as she believed in the truth, she felt she had no choice but to bow to his superior wisdom of the masculine point of view.

"And what about you?" she asked. If he let them believe he was the baby's father, the next logical conclusion was that he'd slept with her before they'd married. "There could be another shiner in your future."

He lifted his shoulders in a dismissive gesture. "Right now, the worst they'll believe is that we had to get married because you were pregnant." He grinned suddenly, the smile that could bring her to her knees. Her heart gave a painful lurch. "Guys, especially the Marchetti brothers, understand stuff like that. I'm prepared to accept responsibility for this baby in every way."

"You are the world's sweetest man."

"Good God, don't spread that lie around."

She moved in front of him and stood on tiptoe to cup his face in her hands. He needed a shave. His whiskers scraped her palms as she brought his mouth down to hers. Her crush on him had never been more staggering. "You would be a wonderful father," she blurted.

He started to shake his head, but she kissed him. His arms came around her as he straightened, then lifted her off the floor. His breathing went from normal to ragged in one point two seconds and hers wasn't far behind. The next thing she knew, he'd set her down and taken two steps back as he ran a shaking hand through his hair. She wanted to drop kick his self-control into the nearest trash compactor.

"I don't know the first thing about raising a kid," he said, his voice not quite as steady as normal.

"Neither do I. But your instinct to protect this child is a very good start."

An angry frown twisted his handsome face. "Don't make me into something I'm not."

"Okay. As long as you take your own advice. Don't make yourself into a bad guy. My God, Steve, you're putting my family first."

"It's no big deal."

He was wrong. His selflessness was a very big deal. He was making a sacrifice that would change his life forever. She had to try one more time to talk him out of it. "Let me tell them the truth."

"Why? They've accepted everything and drawn their own conclusions. They're very happy. I see no reason to rock the boat."

"What about Nick? If past behavior is any gauge, he'll go ballistic."

A shadow stole into his eyes. "He'll understand."

Steve looked at the clock on his office wall— 8:00 a.m. His eyes felt grainy, as if he'd walked through a sandstorm with them open. In a way he had. Life with Rosie was one storm after another. He was doing his best to get through with everything intact. But there was still time to mess up. Way too many nights of Rosie in her nightgown, barefoot and pregnant. What if he didn't have the strength to keep from holding her in his arms? Kissing her. Wanting her. Not being able to have her. He wasn't sure how much more he could take.

He marked this marriage the same way she counted her pregnancy—in weeks. His torture seemed shorter that way. As a boy, he'd constantly wished his background had been different. Then he'd grown up and decided it was a waste of time, not to mention energy thinking about what he couldn't change. Until Rosie.

Take this morning for instance. He'd awakened at the crack of dawn, fresh from a dream of kissing Rosie. Then he remembered the real thing and his thoughts escalated from there. She was just on the other side of the wall, and knowing that had made sleep impossible. Facing her so soon after wanting her so badly was asking for trouble. He'd left the apartment and stopped at his condo to shower for work.

Now in his office, with the door slightly ajar, he heard the outer one open. He glanced at the clock again—8:10 a.m. It was pretty early for his secretary, but they were busy. There was a lot of corporate activity in the first quarter of the year, personnel shifting, which meant work filtered to him for background checks. Maybe Sandy had decided to come in and catch up a bit before she got sidetracked with the phones. He appreciated her dedication, but hoped she wasn't doing it at the expense of her personal life.

Only he was allowed to do that.

"You know you're not supposed to be here yet," he called out.

The door opened and Nick Marchetti stood there. "Who were you expecting?" he asked.

"My secretary."

"The tall blonde?"

"Yeah. Thanks for sending her to me. She's very efficient."

Nick glanced at his watch. "Do you always expect her before business hours?"

Steve's first thought when he'd seen his friend was a flash of hope that he was here to patch things up. Nick's sarcastic tone crushed that.

Steve stood and moved from behind his desk. "What do you want, Nick?"

His black eyes burned with intensity even as his voice remained steady. This Nick Marchetti was too calm for the man Steve knew so well.

"You don't look any different," Nick said.

"What's that supposed to mean?"

"I've known you for over twenty years, but I just found out I don't know you at all."

"You talked to your folks." It wasn't a question. He knew about the baby.

"You underhanded son of a bitch. All this time I never realized what a scheming manipulator you are. I told you my sister had split up with the weasel and you couldn't wait to sleep with her."

"That's not what happened."

"No?" One black eyebrow raised questioningly. "She's pregnant. I've been around the block enough to know she didn't get that way by spontaneous combustion."

"Of course not, but—"

"You and I were supposed to keep her safe from the bad guys. When did you turn into one?"

"It wasn't like that. Nick, you're my friend—"

"Friends don't do this." The other man pointed an accusing finger. "We had an understanding. Or did you plan this from the first? When Rosie was most vulnerable, you moved in for the kill?''

There was an element of truth in everything Nick said. Steve knew there was little point in defending himself. No matter what, he was damned. He *had* slept with Rosie.

"I'm the same as I've always been, Nick," he said coldly. "The dirty kid from the county home that your parents took under their wing."

"I never cared about that."

"Right. I believe you," he said. He could play at sarcasm, too.

Steve glared at him. There was no point in prolonging this. He planted his feet wide apart and lifted his chin slightly. "You get one more shot, Nick. One freebie, then I defend myself. We both know you're no match for gutter trash like me. Take your *best* shot, or get the hell out of my office."

Breathing hard, Nick met his gaze for several long moments. Then he shook his head. "I just wanted you to know that I finally get what a cheating bastard you are. I love my sister. Unfortunately she showed the poor judgment to marry you. Consider this a warning—if you hurt Rosie, in any way, I'll get you, Schafer." He turned and walked toward the door. Stopping, he glanced over his shoulder. "And it'll be a lot more than one shot."

Rosie pressed the elevator up button in Steve's office building. She'd overslept that morning and found him gone when she woke up. Gone without the work he'd brought home. It might be important. She clutched his briefcase tightly in her hand, firmly reminding herself that this was *not* an excuse to see him.

Her stomach lurched in direct proportion to the speed of her vertical ascent. She tolerated elevators only slightly better than airplanes, but it was the quickest, easiest method of getting where she wanted to go. No way was she walking up fifty-one flights to Steve's office. What was it about men that made them want to be on the top floor?

When the car reached its destination, the doors whispered open and she stepped out onto the plush hunter green carpet. It had been a long time since her last visit here. She had learned to treat Steve the same way she did high-calorie desserts. Avoidance. Why torture yourself by looking at what you couldn't have?

Now she was married to him. For a few more weeks she had to see him odd hours of the day and night. She felt her self-control slipping. Like last night.

A shiver coursed through her as she thought about their kiss. When he'd pulled her close, she'd been so sure he wanted her. Then he pushed her away and she found out she was wrong. So wrong. She tried to ignore the little stab of pain as she looked around.

"Classy, Schafer," she said, nodding with approval. She'd forgotten how swank.

She knew he had the entire floor for his offices. There was a large mahogany desk in the center of the reception area. No one manned the station, so she bypassed it and made her way to Steve's office.

The door was open a crack, so she went in. He was there with a tall, attractive blonde. Standing side by side, shoulders brushing, they were looking over some papers on his desk and neither noticed her. This was not the frumpy, middle-aged assistant she'd once met. This was her worst nightmare, a flashback to the most humiliating moment of her entire life.

Why did a strong visual send you hurtling back in time to feel the same bad feelings? She was an awkward eighteen-year-old again. Earlier that evening, Steve had bounced her boyfriend for getting too free with his hands. During the confrontation, he'd looked at her and she thought she'd recognized a hunger in his eyes—for her. She had decided to be a woman of action and find out. A short while later she'd found out, all right.

She'd stood in the doorway to his condo face to face with Steve, bare-chested and wearing boxers. He'd looked at her as if she had purple hair. Behind him was a tall tousle-haired blonde in nothing but his shirt and a cat-who-ate-the-canary smile. Rosie had prayed that the earth would swallow her whole. But even then she'd somehow known that wouldn't be enough to erase the humiliating moment.

Time wasn't the answer, either. Because she felt exactly the same now as she had then—pounding heart, shaky knees and sweaty palms. And don't forget trembling mouth. She had to get out of there.

She must have made some noise because Steve and the woman she assumed to be his secretary simultaneously looked up.

"Rosie. What are you doing here?"

Was it her imagination or did he sound guilty? She was thinking like a wife. Her mistake. He had been nothing but honest about what this marriage would be. She had no reason to expect anything more. If she repeated that mantra a hundred times, a thousand times, maybe her brain would absorb the message.

She set his briefcase down just inside the doorway. "You forgot this."

He stood and walked over to her. "Are you all right?"

"Fine." She caught her top lip between her teeth to stop the quivering.

"You didn't have to come all the way downtown. I could have sent a messenger over to the apartment."

"I—I thought there might be something important that you needed."

He stared at her. "You're white as a sheet. Come over here and sit down."

His fingers curling around her elbow felt warm through the silky material of her loose-fitting top as he guided her to the chair in front of his desk. Rosie didn't sit. She already felt short and didn't want to increase her disadvantage.

Steve glanced at the blonde. "Ro, I don't think you've met my secretary. This is Sandy Benedict. Sandy, this is my wife, Rosie."

The woman smiled with genuine warmth and held out her hand. "It's a pleasure to meet you, Mrs. Schafer."

"The pleasure's mine," Rosie answered, squeezing the other woman's fingers.

Rosie met her gaze and realized how far she had to tip her head back to make eye contact. There were many times in her life when she had wished that she'd caught one of the Marchetti genes for height, but never more than now. This woman was five ten, if she was an inch. Her professional business suit didn't hide her fantastic legs, and Rosie knew—the way a woman knows these things—that her shade of honey-blond didn't come from a bottle.

Rosie smoothed a hand over her abdomen and faced the fact that if this was a competition she was in no condition to race. She would never be tall. With enough peroxide and tint she could be blond, but she would look like a streetwalker. But even more than her looks, there was something that set her apart. Something that took her out of any real or imagined contest. Something that all the vertical stripes in the world couldn't disguise.

She was pregnant—with another man's child.

She had no illusions about their marriage. She had no right to expect him to curb his natural inclinations. Steve worked twelve-hour days and she assumed at least eight or even ten were spent with this beautiful woman. Rosie had never felt so short and round and insignificant than she did at this moment.

Steve stared at her. "Are you sure you're all right?"

"Never better," she lied, forcing cheerfulness into her voice.

"Can I get you a glass of water, Mrs. Schafer?" Sandy asked.

"Yes, thank you."

The woman moved to the door with catlike grace. Rosie knew her own stride bordered on a waddle. Ducks were never described as light-footed, nimble, willowy, or sophisticated. She'd never heard anyone envied or admired for ducklike gracefulness.

"What's wrong, Ro?"

Her gaze snapped to his where she read concern. "I'm just tired."

"Maybe you should take the afternoon off and catch a nap."

"I might just do that."

If only she could snooze through the rest of her pregnancy and wake up when her baby was born. She could be the opposite of the fairy tales she'd always read. Go to sleep and instead of her handsome prince breaking the spell, when she awoke, he would be gone.

Then she could pick up the pieces of her life, mend her broken heart and stop hoping for something that was never going to happen.

Chapter Ten

Eight weeks after promising to take full responsibility for the baby, Steve followed Rosie into the dark apartment and flipped on the lights. They had just returned from their final childbirth class and Rosie had sworn she needed a crane to get her up the stairs. She carefully lowered herself to the love seat.

"I can't believe we're finished," he said, sitting beside her.

She scooted over until the sofa arm stopped her. "I can."

He hadn't realized the major stumbling block to his vow of responsibility would be Rosie herself. She had resisted when Steve had offered to be her labor coach. He had persuaded her with his usual rationale—it would make everyone suspicious if he didn't. So he'd accompanied her to the six-week course and learned how to help her through the birth.

It seemed like yesterday that he'd found out about her predicament. The time had passed surprisingly swiftly. Maybe because this was the best life he'd ever had. Nothing spectacular. Work during the day, dinner at home, sleep in separate beds. But Rosie made every minute special.

It was killing him. There was no way to change his past into something worthy of Rosie, and very soon now he faced a future without her.

"I can't believe your due date is just three weeks away," he said, pleased that his voice revealed nothing.

Rosie looked down at her stomach and smiled wryly. "I can." She sighed wistfully. "I can't believe my figure will ever be back to normal."

He had to admit he missed her lush curves, but she had never looked more beautiful to him than she did right now—very pregnant and on the brink of motherhood. The closer they got to zero hour, thoughts crossed his mind that he'd never expected to have. Could he cut it as a dad? Or was he like his old man, the type to disappear, never trying to be a husband or a father?

He would never make forever-after promises to Rosie because he was afraid he couldn't keep them.

He noticed the way she leaned away from him, her body language screaming "Keep your distance." Ever since the day she'd dropped into his office, she had been reserved, remote, with little resemblance to the Rosie who wore her heart on her sleeve. She'd gone away somehow and he wasn't sure where or why. It should have eased his concerns about her being okay after they split up. But her behavior worried him. This was so unlike her cheery, upbeat self. The Rosie he knew and...

His next thought was "loved," but he skidded to

a stop. He couldn't go there. As Nick had so eloquently reminded him that day in his office, you could take a kid out of the gutter, but you couldn't take the gutter out of the kid. That's why he'd wanted Steve to stay away from his sister in the first place. But Steve's gutter mentality had overpowered his self-control. He'd stepped over the line—married and slept with Rosie.

Since that day, he and Nick hadn't spoken. If the Marchettis had business with him, one of the other brothers handled it. The friendship was over, gone—kaput—as if it had never existed.

Steve tried not to think about that. When the thought intruded, he did his best to ignore the ache in his gut. He missed his friend.

He watched Rosie shift her position on the couch. Her baby-enhanced abdomen made it hard for her to get comfortable. Soon she would be gone, too. The ache increased tenfold and expanded into full-blown pain that he couldn't overlook. He'd been a fool to believe he had nothing to lose by marrying her. The time they'd spent together had changed him. She'd added color and texture to his life. Companionship, humor, and caring.

If he had known how bad this would hurt, would he have gone through with this crazy scheme to give her his name as a shield? In a heartbeat, came his answer. It had always been the right thing to do.

"I'll take your silence as agreement," she said.

"Of what?" He'd been lost in thought. "What did you say?"

"That you think my figure will never be back to normal."

"Do you want to know what I was really thinking?" he asked.

"Sure. I'm tough. I have four brothers who have the collective sensitivity of a bull elephant. There's nothing you can say to me that will penetrate the thick, armadillo-like skin that I've spent years perfecting. I will—"

He leaned over and placed his finger over her lips, silencing her. For several moments he just looked his fill at her, memorizing her features for the times when he couldn't. He knew she wasn't as thick-skinned as she pretended. The humor protected her tender heart. He wanted to leave her with more than his name. He wanted to give her the knowledge that she was a beautiful, desirable woman.

The soft living room lights bathed her in a glow. Dark curls danced around her shoulders. One corner of her full, sensuous mouth curved up.

He cupped her chin in his palm and rubbed her cheek with his thumb. "May lightning strike me if this isn't the truth. I was just thinking that you have never looked more lovely than you do right now."

She blinked. "As compared to who? Broomhilda?"

"As compared to no one. You are unique, Ro."

Her big brown eyes sparkled with unshed tears. "You're lying through your teeth, but I'm going to disregard that and choose to believe you. B-because I'm a blimp and I w-want to."

He took her face in both hands and brushed the trickling tears away with his thumbs. "When are you going to stop putting yourself down and get the message that you are a knockout?"

"When pigs fly."

"I'm serious, Ro."

"So am I. Desirable to whom? You?" Her look told him she knew the answer to that. He couldn't say the words he wanted to, so he kissed her.

When he pulled away, her gaze moved over his face. She curled her fingers around his wrist and said, "When are you going to stop believing that no one could care about you? You're not the blackguard Nick thinks you are."

Her choice of words took the sting out of them and he couldn't stop the half smile. But he was as bad as Nick thought him. He always had been. There had never been a time since meeting Rosie that he didn't want her—including now.

He slid close and put his arm around her, pulling her to his side. He felt her resistance melt away and she rested her cheek on his chest. His shirt grew wet from her tears.

"Don't cry."

"I can't seem to help it lately. Songs on the radio make me blubber like a baby. There's no rhyme or reason to it. Just hormones." She shifted restlessly.

"Are you uncomfortable?"

"My back. I was on my feet a lot today in the store."

"Turn around. I'll rub it for you."

She looked up at him and smiled. "Sainthood is yours. Saint Steve has the ring of alliteration to it."

He braced her with a hand on her shoulder, and put his palm on the small of her back, rubbing in a sort of circular pressing motion. She sighed in contentment. "Saint Steve Schafer, marvelous masseuse and master— Ahh," she sighed contentedly.

He continued the ministrations until she leaned

against him, letting the back of her head rest on his chest. He put his arms around her, tenderly cradling her swollen belly.

"The baby's moving a lot," she said.

"I can feel him." He thought for a minute. "Do you think he can hear what we're saying?"

"I've read that they can. Although how anyone knows for sure since babies can't come out and respond to a survey, is beyond me."

He held her and leaned slightly forward, aiming his words toward her tummy. "Okay, kid. I just want to let you know that everything is okay. You're safe. Your grandparents and uncles are looking forward to meeting you. There are lots of people who love you. You've got the best mom in the world."

"With a family like that, he won't even miss a dad," she said wistfully. "I wonder if Wayne ever thinks about us."

"I'm sure he does. He cared about you, Ro." What could the lie hurt? She never had to know that she was just a means to an end for the two-bit hustler. There was no way she could find out—

He went still. The pictures? No. Surely her mother had disposed of the report he'd given her. He had to make sure. Tomorrow he would—

"Damn."

"What is it?" she asked, straightening as she turned to look at him.

"I just forgot something. My trip." He was leaving on a crack-of-dawn flight. No way could he see Mrs. M. then. He would phone her when he had a chance. Steve looked at her. "Are you going to be all right alone while I'm out of town next week?"

"Of course. I'm a big girl. I'm an—"

"Independent woman. Yeah, yeah. I know the drill."

"Then my work here is done," she said with a grin.

"I still don't like the idea of leaving you by yourself at this point in the pregnancy."

"Then I'll tell you one more time why I don't want to stay with my parents." She held up her hand to count off the reasons on her fingers. "My mother is busy with preparations for the baby shower. I'm more comfortable here in my own place. They drive me crazy with don't-you-feel-anything-yet phone calls. Up close and personal for a week would be too much. If anything happens, I can call someone, or in the worst case scenario, I'll call a cab. Or 9-1-1."

"I don't like this. I'll put off the trip."

She shook her head. "No way. This is your moment of glory. You've worked to get this account for months."

"I'll send someone else—"

"They want you, Steve. You're the best. Don't worry. Like you said, I'm not due for another three weeks. Besides, first babies are always late."

"My luck isn't that good."

"Your luck?" She laughed. "I'm the one big as a house with child. If it were up to me, I'd go now. But my theory is that the longer he's in there, the better it is for him when he comes out."

"That does it." He pointed at her. "Promise me you'll hold off the birth until I get back."

She held up her hand, palm out. "I swear."

Following her mother's explicit instructions, Rosie drove through to the alley and pulled into the garage at the rear of her parents' property. That way it would be easier to load the loot into her car after the baby shower today. She was very early for the festivities, but had felt restless sitting around her apartment waiting to go. She wished it was over because she just didn't feel like it. Her back had ached all morning and party mood wasn't in her vocabulary today.

Steve had been gone a week. It was a sneak preview of what it would be like when he was out of her life for good. She hadn't liked what she saw. It wasn't just loneliness, although she'd missed him terribly. But he made her happy, just by being there. Like the missing piece to a jigsaw puzzle, he had filled the hole in her soul, made her complete. She was afraid to give a name to what she felt, because there was only one word she could think of. She wouldn't say it; she couldn't bring herself to think it. There was another four-letter word that would describe him soon enough: g-o-n-e.

She opened the rear gate, then walked past the pool to the house. The back door was locked. While she rummaged in her purse for the key, Rosie felt a twinge in her back. Must have spent too much time on her feet pacing the apartment. Soon she could sit and be the center of attention. There were a million and one things she would rather do, all of them with Steve.

But the lure of the sweet baby things she would receive was irresistible. After the ultrasound, she had decided not to find out the baby's sex. She didn't regret her decision, but there was the matter of nursery furniture. She'd put two sets on layaway—one for a boy and one for a girl. If she wasn't so determined to preserve the surprise, everything would be ready.

She recalled her shock when Steve had volunteered to shop with her. Considering his resistance to the pastime, she gave him an A for going above and beyond the call of duty. She was glad he would be back today and the apartment wouldn't be empty when she went home later that night.

Rosie unlocked the door and let herself into the kitchen. Two ladies bustled around preparing food. She looked at the two strangers, one a tall brunette, the other smaller with pixie-cut blond hair. "I suppose you could tell that the shower's for me."

The short woman nodded as she smiled. "We noticed."

"Is there something I can do to help?" Rosie asked politely.

Both ladies shook their heads firmly. The tall one said, "You just go on in, and find your mother. Relax and have a good time. This is your day."

"Thanks." Rosie started for the doorway. It wasn't like Flo Marchetti not to be in the thick of things, directing traffic. "Do you know where she is?"

The blonde looked thoughtful for a moment. "She disappeared right after a man showed up. I think she took him into her office."

"Thanks. I'll find her."

That was odd, Rosie thought as she walked down the long hall toward her mother's room at the front of the house. Who could be there? Her father and brothers had gone pale when she'd teased them about coming to a baby shower. They had made plans to be out doing something manly today, no doubt an activity that involved sweating and grunting. She couldn't wait to see the man with her mother, the one brave enough to chance a houseful of cackling women.

Her back spasmed again as she walked through the family room, and she stopped to rub it as she caught her breath. Whose idea was it to make a house this big? she thought crossly.

Voices drifted to her as she got closer. She recognized her mother's, and the man's sounded familiar. But it couldn't be. He wasn't due home until tonight.

"I forgot all about these until a week ago." Steve? It *was* him. "You were never home when I called, and this wasn't something I wanted to leave on a message machine."

"I'm not surprised." That was her mother. "Are you sure it's a good idea to destroy them? What if he comes back—"

"He won't. These prove his only interest in Rosie was financial. He got what he wanted. Money. Rosie is safe."

What in God's name were they talking about? Destroy what? Whose interest in her? Could they be talking about Wayne? Why, after all these months?

She rounded the corner and stopped in the doorway. Her mother sat behind her desk. Steve stood beside her looking down at something. He glanced up and without missing a beat shoved what looked like pictures into a manila envelope.

"Hey, squirt," he said.

"Hi, yourself." She moved into the room and stopped directly in front of the desk.

"Rosie!" Her mother looked shocked. "You're early."

"There's a lot of that going around. I didn't expect you until tonight," she said to Steve.

"I finished my business and caught the first available flight out."

A part of her mind registered the fact that he looked tired. She wanted to wrap her arms around him and welcome him home and say how much she'd missed her husband. Another part of her vibrated with the need to know what was going on here. What was in that envelope that would prove anything?

Recovering her composure with an effort, Flo stood. "I'm glad you're so early, Rosie. Let me show you the shower decorations in the living room."

"In a minute." Without warning, she reached out and snatched the envelope before they could stop her. "But first I'd like to see what you and Steve find so fascinating."

He lifted a hand to take it from her. "It's nothing, Ro. Just business. Why don't you go with Mrs. M. and—"

"No," she said, backing away. She'd heard the expression "waiting for the other shoe to fall," but had never understood it more keenly than this moment.

She upended the envelope and photographs spilled out onto the desk. Grabbing one, she saw that it was Wayne in a passionate clinch with a woman. There was no question that it wasn't Rosie. The stranger was blonde. She picked up another that showed the couple arm in arm coming out of a restaurant decorated for Christmas, then another with them entering a motel room. There was no mistaking the timing. Wayne had asked her to marry him a week after Thanksgiving.

It took about three seconds for Rosie to figure out the scenario. Steve's private investigator had tailed Wayne and came up with this evidence that Wayne was playing her for a fool. Not aware of her pregnancy, her mother had sent Steve to buy him off.

"The meddling Marchettis strike again," she said under her breath. She felt as if she'd been slapped, but it had nothing to do with Wayne. She had never cared about him enough to hurt like this. It was so much worse than she could ever have imagined. Steve had witnessed every humiliating moment of her life, but this was the topper.

"Mother, I'd like to speak to Steve alone."

"Rosie, honey—"

"Please, Ma."

The older woman nodded and reluctantly left the room.

Her back spasmed again, but she ignored it as she looked at Steve. "I suppose you feel validated. You have hard-copy proof that you're not the only man who doesn't want me."

"Rosie, listen—"

"Let's call a spade a spade. Any feelings you have for me are pity, pure and simple."

"I never felt sorry for you."

Shock was the only explanation for the fact that she was still standing. She couldn't afford to let the pain in. But she had to know the truth.

"Then explain why you made love to me. What other motivation could there be for those kisses? You made it clear from the beginning that the marriage would have a beginning and an end. Did the middle include tossing me a few crumbs of self-esteem so you wouldn't get bored?"

"That never entered my mind." He came around the desk and reached for her.

"Don't touch me," she said, backing away. The pain was starting and she didn't want to feel it. That much misery couldn't be good for her, but especially not for the baby. "You made love to me and I hoped we had a chance. You kissed me and I kept alive the dream that I could make you care for me. But it was pity. All the time you just felt sorry for poor Rosie Marchetti."

"Rosie, don't cry. Listen to me, squirt—"

"Don't call me that!" She glared at him in spite of the tears rolling down her cheeks. Angrily she wiped away the moisture. "I hate when you call me that."

"We have to talk."

"There's nothing to say." She held up a finger. "No, wait. I owe you thanks for letting the baby and I borrow your last name. I just don't understand the song and dance about us living together. And this business of saving my brothers from themselves. I don't get it. What was that—"

A sudden grinding pain started in her back and tightened all the way around her abdomen. The agony doubled her over.

She squeezed hard when Steve took her hands. "Rosie? Is it the baby?"

Unable to speak through the contraction, she nodded.

"Oh, God," he said. "It's too early. This is my fault."

Then he lifted her in his arms. Through a haze of pain and fear, she heard him call for her mother and explain that he was taking her to the hospital. He carried her out front to his car, all the while muttering that she had to be all right. He was the world's biggest ass.

Rosie leaned back against the seat, resting. She welcomed the physical pain. She harnessed her strength. She needed to focus all her energy on having her baby.

It took her mind off Steve and the hard-copy proof that he didn't love her.

Chapter Eleven

Steve stood by the hospital bed as Rosie held her new baby. Watching her cradle her daughter, wrapped up cocoon-like with her tiny head covered in a pink-and-blue knit cap, he swallowed the lump in his throat. After about twelve hours she'd given birth, and now he knew why it was called labor. If he could have taken her pain himself, he would have.

Seeing her go through that had been the hardest thing he'd ever done. It had pushed away all their problems and pulled them together, united in their efforts to bring this precious child into the world. All the while Rosie had worked, he had been so afraid that the shock and upset of seeing those pictures had made the baby come too early. And because of that, something might happen to the baby, and Rosie.

"How do you feel?" he asked.

"I'm sore, but I feel—" She stopped and he could tell she was searching for the words. "This is the most wonderful experience I've ever had. No wonder

my mother was so anxious to have grandchildren.''
She looked up at him. ''What am I going to name
her? The baby I mean, not my mother.''

Steve rubbed his eyes, then ran a hand through his
hair. He hadn't slept for two days. He'd taken an earlier flight to get home as soon as possible, then he'd
decided to get back those damn pictures before going
home to Rosie.

During the week he'd been gone, he'd thought
about her and how he hated being away from her.
More than once he'd thought about telling her what
was in his heart and had finally decided there would
be no peace until he did. But after seeing those damn
pictures, she'd come to her own conclusions, all of
them bad. She wouldn't believe that he loved her.
He'd never seen her that upset. If anything had happened to her or the baby... He couldn't even think
about that.

He would never have forgiven himself.

Thank God everything had gone textbook perfect,
but now the adrenaline was wearing off. He felt like
roadkill and probably looked worse. But Rosie was
the one who had done all the work and she looked
amazing. He'd never seen her more beautiful. The
sight of her, with love shining in her eyes, unable to
stop looking at the baby, was the most incredible
thing he'd ever seen. Instinct, fierce and furious, tightened his gut. He wanted to wrap his arms around both
of them and keep the bad stuff away.

If any guy ever hurt that little baby girl the way he
had Rosie, he would hunt him down and make him
pay. Was this the way Nick felt, trying to protect his
sister from someone like himself? The light went on
in his weary mind. No wonder her brother had reacted

so intensely to the news of their marriage and then the baby.

"What am I going to name her?" Rosie said again, looking at him in a panic. "I was so sure she was going to be a boy."

Steve congratulated himself. Not once did he wince at the "I's" in those two sentences. Not even a twitch. He'd given up the right to be part of her life. He would never forget the anger in her eyes when she'd said he had hard-copy proof that no man wanted her. Every fiber of his being vibrated with the need to tell her how much—how *long*—he'd wanted her. Now she wouldn't believe him, and the shadow of hurt he'd seen in Rosie's face would haunt him forever.

"Is she all right?" He stood beside the bed, staring down at the baby.

"The pediatrician says she's fine." Rosie looked up at him, her beautiful eyes glowing with excitement. "You went into the newborn nursery while they checked her over. What did they say?"

He stuck his fingertips into the pockets of his jeans. "That she's perfect. But I thought—" He shrugged.

He was still half afraid that there would be repercussions for Rosie and the baby from going into labor before her due date.

"What? They have no reason to lie to you."

Unlike some people. Meaning him. She didn't say it in so many words, but he heard it.

"I've never been this close to a baby. If this ever gets out, I'll deny it, but that little girl scares me to death."

Rosie smiled down at the sweet bundle in her arms. He wanted to tell her why he'd kept the pictures from her. That his only excuse was to prevent her any more pain. But he'd messed up. More proof that Nick was right and he wasn't the man for her. He would never hurt her again. The last best gift he would give Nick and Rosie was to walk away from her.

That thought sent pain careening through him. He had never wished to be a better man more than he did right now. Rosie's struggle to bring a new life into the world had taught him the meaning of the word respect. No matter how much it would hurt, he would disappear and let her find someone who was her equal.

The privacy curtain around Rosie's bed moved slightly and Steve saw Liz Anderson, the short, dark-haired obstetrics nurse who had guided them through labor and delivery. Wearing rose-colored hospital scrubs, she studied mother and baby and nodded with satisfaction.

She looked at him. "There are three burly men out here who stated categorically that designated visiting hours are for everyone but them. They threatened to pick me up bodily and lock me in the broom closet."

Rosie laughed. "Their name doesn't happen to be Marchetti, does it?"

The woman nodded. "One of them *thinks* he's very charming."

"Joe?" Rosie and Steve asked together.

"That's the one," the nurse said, laughing.

Rosie tucked her curly hair behind her ear. "He's harmless."

"That's what I told him." Then her grin disappeared and she was all business again. "I'll bend the rules since I have a feeling it would take the National Guard to keep them out." She half turned, then shot them a stern look over her shoulder. She reminded Steve of a mother lion protecting her cubs. "But keep it short, about two minutes. And, by the way, your parents left. They were tired after being up all night. Your mother said she would be back later." She looked at Steve and a glint stole into her eyes. "It'll cost you, but I promise not to tell them how this little girl scares you."

"Aren't there laws against eavesdropping?"

"A hospital is a law unto itself," she said loftily.

Rosie grinned. "Send in the burlies."

Liz nodded and left. Moments later Alex, Joe, and Luke Marchetti stood shoulder to shoulder on one side of their sister. Rosie angled her elbow and her body slightly forward so they could get a good look at their new niece.

Alex met his gaze across the bed. "Congratulations, Pop. How does it feel to be a dad?"

"Pretty amazing," Steve answered truthfully. That was no lie, no act. He couldn't imagine feeling more protective, more anxious, or more love if the baby had been his own.

"What are you going to name her?" Joe asked. "You might want to give some thought to Josephine."

"What about Lucinda?" Luke said. "I think it has a nice ring to it."

Alex loosely draped his arm across his younger brother's shoulders. "What do you think of Alexandra Josephine—"

"Florence Thomasina?" Rosie laughed. "She's no bigger than a minute and that's a lot of name to pin on her."

"No problem. She's a Marchetti," Alex said. "Ma said she looks just like you when you were a baby."

Luke met Steve's gaze. "She's a Schafer, too."

"Yeah," Steve said, seeing something he didn't understand in the other man's eyes. In every way that counts, this baby *is* mine, he thought.

"I haven't decided on a name yet," Rosie said. "But you guys will be the first to know when I do." Frowning, she looked past them. "Where's Nick? Does he know about her?"

The three men exchanged uncomfortable looks. Alex finally spoke up. "He knows. But there's a business crisis. He made sure you and the munchkin were all right, and said he'll see you when he can."

"Oh."

There was a world of hurt in that one small word and Steve knew he was responsible for it. Rosie and Nick had always had a special bond. Her oldest brother had shared all the major events in her life. It didn't get more major than giving birth, and Nick wasn't there.

Steve knew no business crisis in the world could have kept Nick away. It was him, Steve. It had everything to do with who he was and where he came from. He would give anything if he could change that. Rosie was his wife and today she had made them a family. This is what life was all about. He had come to need her more than he thought possible.

The nurse came around the curtain again. "Visiting hours are over. Time for the Marchetti marauders to hit the road."

Joe elbowed past Luke and Alex to stand over the petite nurse. He stooped slightly to read her name tag. "Ms. E. Anderson."

She looked up at him and arched a brow. "Impressive."

He grinned. "Think so?"

"I do. Reading is an underrated skill. You should do it more often."

"Look," he said, frowning, "we'd like to spend a little more time with our new niece. She's the first—"

"No. You look, Marchetti. This is a hospital. There are rules. Rules are for everyone. Including you. Either go quietly—"

"Or you'll call security?"

She shook her head. "I don't have to." In the blink of an eye, she reached up and snagged his ear, yanking firmly. Joe yelped, but she didn't let go. "Now follow me."

"'Bye, sis. Nice-lookin' kid...." His voice faded as he left the room.

The last two Marchetti brothers grinned as they shook Steve's hand. Alex said, "I guess it's time to go."

Luke bent and kissed Rosie's cheek. "We'll see you when the pit bull goes off duty."

Rosie nodded. "Thanks for coming. I love you."

"Same here, sis," they said together.

Then Steve was alone with Rosie. He watched her shift uncomfortably in the bed.

"Are you okay?"

"Just tired. And sore," she answered. She looked at him uncertainly.

"What, Ro?"

"Could you put the baby in her little isolette for me?"

Steve hadn't held her yet. He'd taken parenting classes with Rosie, but now was his baptism of fire.

"Sure," he said with more confidence than he felt. Rosie laid the infant in his outstretched arms. He settled her comfortably in the crook of his left elbow.

She felt so sweet and small and warm—a living, breathing miracle. The lump of emotion was back. The feelings were so big, so powerful, so profound that he was caught off guard. With his free hand, he rubbed his eyes. He swung away and set the baby in her little square bed, on her side, as they'd been taught.

"Do you think she's comfortable in this thing?" he asked. When he turned to Rosie, he saw that she was looking at him strangely, smiling slightly.

"What?" he asked.

"I was just wondering what the Macho Men of America would say about breaking the cardinal rule. You remember, number one or two, the one about tears in your eyes."

"I wasn't— It's not what you—"

"Sell it somewhere else, Schafer. It's exactly what I think, and just about the sweetest thing I've ever seen," she finished, her own voice catching with emotion.

"Okay. There's a corollary to the rule book. During and immediately following a life-altering experience such as birth, all rules are null and void."

Rosie had never loved him more. She was still mad at him, but she couldn't help loving him. She always had and always would. Her own eyes filled with tears, of sadness and joy. In front of her brothers, he had claimed her child as his own. His unselfishness had never meant more than it did at this moment.

He gave his heart freely, simply and purely for the sake of a child. She knew this because he could have walked away. Instead, he'd chosen not just to be there, but help her through.

"I wouldn't have made it without you, Steve."

He sat in the chair by the bed and hesitated before taking her hand. "I didn't do anything."

She shook her head. "I was ready to give up. Then you made me look at you and told me I could do this. You made me believe."

He glanced at the sleeping infant. "I like it when I'm right."

"I will always be grateful to you for my child."

He would leave soon and the baby was all she would have.

A few hours later, smiling from ear to ear, Flo Marchetti breezed into her hospital room. While she looked at the peacefully sleeping baby in the isolette, Rosie tried to hide the tears streaming down her face. But she should have known better. Mama Marchetti sees all, knows all, and what she doesn't see and know, she guesses with amazing accuracy.

Flo pulled the chair closer to the bed and sat. "Tell your mother what's wrong."

"Hormones."

"Body chemistry does not work against you when your life is perfect." The older woman shook her head. "You have everything you always wanted. A beautiful, healthy baby girl. She looks just like you did when you were a baby. My granddaughter— But I digress. You have a man who adores you." She stopped and stared. "Which part of what I just said are you looking at me like that for?"

"The part where the man adores me." Rosie

twisted her fingers together. "Ma, I have a confession." She hesitated. "I have two confessions."

Her mother touched a finger to her chin in a thoughtful gesture. "Let me guess. You and Steve married because you were pregnant. And he's not the father."

Rosie's eyes widened. "How did you know?"

"That Tahoe wedding had 'shotgun' written all over it. But I wasn't certain until you told us about the pregnancy. Then the pieces fell into place."

"Why didn't you tell me you knew?"

"You always accuse me of meddling." She shrugged. "It was a matter of pride."

"Does Daddy know?" Rosie asked.

Flo shook her head. "And I see no point in telling him, or your brothers, either."

"Why?"

"For the same reason Steve let us believe the conclusion we jumped to about him being the baby's father. Protecting the Marchetti men from themselves."

"Is there anything you don't know?" Rosie asked.

Her mother nodded. "I have no idea why you're crying."

"Steve doesn't love me."

"You're so wrong."

Rosie vehemently shook her head. "You're mistaking love for pity. Those pictures of Wayne and the bimbo prove it."

"They prove I was right to send Steve to stop the wedding. The real question is why he had them in the first place."

"You hired him to check out Wayne."

This time her mother vehemently shook her head.

"Neither your father nor I asked him to investigate that weasel. Steve did it on his own."

"Why?"

"Rosemarie, you are *not* stupid. I don't understand why this is so hard for you. He *loves* you."

"Now that's where you're wrong, Ma. Not once has he said those words to me."

"Have you told him you love him?"

"Well…" At her mother's narrow-eyed look she squirmed, then blurted, "No."

"Have you given him a hint about how you feel?"

"No."

"So you ran away because he can't read your mind."

"I haven't run anywhere, Mother."

Flo waved a hand. "That was a figure of speech. You are the spoiled youngest of five children. On top of that, the other four are boys who adore you. All your life you've gotten everything you wanted, without asking. The few times you didn't, you went to your room and pouted. It's quite unattractive, dear."

"I'm not doing that."

"Emotionally you are." She folded her hands in her lap and leaned forward earnestly. "Why should he put himself out there if you won't?"

"Because he's the guy."

"He's a guy who's been rejected by the people who should have loved him the most, his parents. May their souls burn in hell," she said angrily. "He can't risk putting his feelings on the line with you. If you throw him away, too, it would destroy him."

"I would never hurt him," Rosie said indignantly. Then she pulled her legs toward her chest and wrapped her arms around them. "And I don't think there's much danger of that. It would only bother him if he loves me.''

"I'm losing my patience, Rosemarie. If he didn't love you, no way in hell would he have married you and led everyone to believe he's the father of your baby. You have to fight for him.'' She leaned forward. "I'm going to tell you a secret. Before I married your father, he was dating someone else. I knew he was the man I wanted to marry, so I told him to drop the bimbo because I loved him more than she ever could.''

"Ma, your language!''

"The point is, you have to fight for your man. Steve needs to know you love him as much as he loves you.'' When Rosie shook her head, her mother's look turned stern. "The truth has been staring you in the face for years. Do you remember when he beat up Timmy Henderson for pushing you off your bike? Or when you were ten and he rigged up the flashlight in your room so we wouldn't know you were reading after lights-out? As far as you were concerned, the word *no* wasn't in his vocabulary. He would do anything to make you happy. He loves you, Rosie. He always has.''

Somehow, hearing her mother say the words put everything into perspective. "I guess I always knew, but I've been afraid to believe. It hurt so much over the years, you know?'' Her mother nodded sympathetically. "Every time I put myself on the line with him, I was turned away.''

Flo looked thoughtful. "That has something to do with Nick. I'm not sure what. But my next mission is to find out and patch those two up.''

"I can save you the trouble, Ma.''

Rosie saw Nick holding the privacy curtain aside as he stood at the foot of her hospital bed. "How long have you been there?" she asked.

"Long enough to know that I'm a narrow-minded moron."

"That's being kind, son." Flo looked at him. "I can't tell you what you really are in front of your sister, my daughter, who's just recovering from childbirth. Suffice it to say it's the rear of a very large animal—"

"I get the picture, Ma." Nick looked at the baby, sound asleep in the isolette. "She's a stunner, my niece."

Rosie smiled softly at her daughter. "How does it feel?"

"Unclehood?" he asked. "Feels great. How long till she's big enough for amusement parks—"

"No. I meant being wrong. It so seldom happens to you. I just wondered how you'd handle it."

"The same way I do everything, with dignity, nobility, style, et cetera."

Rosie shot him a wicked look. "I want viscerals that include words like slime, pond scum, lower than a snake's belly, whatever that stuff is on the underside of rocks at the bottom of lakes where there's no water current to wash it off—"

"Jeez, sis." He held fingertips to palm for a timeout. He looked at his mother. "Isn't it your job to protect and defend your firstborn?"

"Not this time."

"You've both made your point." His look turned serious before he bent to kiss his mother, then Rosie. "I'll see you later."

"Where are you going?" she asked.

"On a mission," he said.

Chapter Twelve

Steve looked around his condo wondering why he'd come here instead of the apartment after leaving the hospital. The tri-level had been professionally decorated. On the main floor was the kitchen, living room, and dining area. Half a flight up were four bedrooms, and six steps down was a large family room that he almost never used. He wondered why the place no longer felt familiar and comfortable. The answer was simple.

Rosie.

She made anywhere home to him, and she hadn't been here. Except the night she'd dropped in and found him with another woman. He'd seen in her eyes then that she would leave him in the dust. That explained why he'd bypassed the apartment. He was already disconnecting, or trying to. Maybe he should have agreed to her suggestion to live here. He would never have brought up the subject of her moving out and she might have just stayed—in spite of marrying him and alienating Nick. Even after seeing those pictures. Yeah, and you could count on snow in July.

The doorbell sounded and his first thought was that bad things came in threes. He'd already listed number one and two and wasn't sure he wanted to face the third.

A vision of Rosie holding the baby flashed into his mind. Before the image of her could draw emotional blood, he opened the door. Surprise didn't quite do justice to what he felt seeing Nick there.

Steve stood in the center of the doorway, blocking it. "What do you want?"

"Aren't you going to invite me in?"

Steve shrugged and stepped aside, then shut the door. It would muffle some of the noise for his neighbors if Nick decided to take his shot now.

"How did you know where to find me?" Steve asked.

"You weren't at the apartment, I figured you'd be here."

So Nick had put some effort into hunting for him. When a guy wanted to hide, it was a disadvantage for someone to know him as well as Nick did. Steve watched his friend reach into the pocket of his suit coat and pull out a cigar.

"What's that for?" he asked, completely mystified.

"It's a good thing you've got me to initiate you into the rituals of fatherhood. When you have a baby, it's customary to hand out cigars to one's friends, acquaintances, brothers-in-law—"

"Fatherhood?"

"Since you dropped the ball on this one, I figured the godfather could pick up the slack and do the cigar bit."

"You're the baby's godfather? Rosie didn't say anything."

"She doesn't know yet. But as the eldest sibling I decided—"

"Time out." Steve made the appropriate gesture with his hands. "You're doing a hell of a lot of figuring and deciding. I don't get it. The last time I saw you, you wanted to cut my heart out with a spoon. What's *your* angle?"

Nick winced at having his own words tossed back at him. "I deserve that. And more. I'll give *you* one shot."

Steve shook his head. "I'm not going to hit you. Not that you don't deserve it."

"You got that right," Nick said ruefully.

"What's going on? Why are you here?"

Nick shoved his hands into his pants pockets and stared at the floor for several moments. He looked up and there was an apologetic expression on his face. "I know everything."

"Define 'everything,'" Steve said suspiciously.

"Why you married Rosie. That the baby isn't yours—"

"I see."

"This is long overdue, buddy. But welcome to the family." He held his hand out.

Steve hesitated. "Why should I believe you?"

Nick shifted uncomfortably. "You have every right to be ticked off. I'm the world's biggest jerk."

"You forgot dumbest."

"What is it with you and Rosie? Groveling isn't hard enough? You two have to heap on the humiliation?"

"You saw Rosie? And the baby?"

Nick nodded. "I just came from there. I overheard her telling mother everything."

"So Mr. and Mrs. M. know, too?"

"I'm not sure about Dad, but Ma does."

"Cheaters never prosper," Steve muttered. He should have known this plan to help Rosie wouldn't go off without a hitch.

"Ma used to tell us that a lot." He met Steve's gaze. "In this case—"

"It's no different. I'm a fraud. Don't worry. The divorce will be kept quiet. I'll support Rosie and my—" He stopped and took a deep breath. "The baby and Rosie won't want for anything."

"Now who's being a dumb jerk?"

"Isn't this what you want? Me out of her life? Ever since we were kids, you made it plain that Rosie was off limits. Any girl was fair game but her."

Nick ran a hand through his dark hair. "I've thought about that a lot. Rosie and I were always close. This sounds really stupid, but as a kid, I think I was jealous that she liked you better."

"You're right. It does sound stupid." Then the meaning of the words sank in. "You sabotaged me?"

"That's about the size of it. Not consciously, but—" Nick shrugged uncomfortably.

"So why would you want me in the family now? Why would you change?"

"I—we haven't changed. The Marchetti family door was always open. You're the one who kept shutting it."

Suddenly Steve understood why Rosie's don't-leave-me-out look had always gotten to him. He understood it. He knew exactly how she felt and hated it—for himself, but especially for her. He had loved her when they were kids, and he was head over heels crazy about her now.

When Steve didn't say anything, Nick went on. "For the record, I would rather see my sister married to you than anyone. We're as close as brothers, in some ways closer—at least we were until I screwed up. I plan to make that up to you. The point is, there's not a doubt in my mind that you'll take care of Rosie. I haven't always been there for her. But you never let her down. I couldn't be happier that you married her. You're one of the good guys, buddy."

Nick held out his hand. Steve knew his friend was telling the truth. The door had always been open. It still was. He could step through, or shut it forever. He grasped Nick's hand firmly, putting everything he felt and couldn't say into it. Then Nick pulled him into a brief backslapping bear hug.

Steve grinned. "You are a jerk."

"Yeah, well..." Nick shuffled his feet. "I know marriage isn't for me and I figured you felt the same way. I was wrong." He grinned. "Better you than me."

Steve grinned, knowing he finally had somewhere to belong. Correction, he'd always had a place, but he'd been too young and stupid and angry to see it. But he did now. He had a shot at everything he'd always wanted. If he blew it, he would be lost forever.

Steve's smile disappeared. "I want this marriage and family, Nick. I love the baby as if she were mine. And I'm nuts about Rosie. But I've hurt her. Badly." He shook his head. "I just don't know how to convince her that I do care."

"You don't have to tell me. I'm a guy. Everything you've done says it loud and clear. But women need to hear the words. And Rosie more than most. For God's sake, she owns a bookstore.''

"Thanks, buddy," Steve said wryly. "I needed more pressure."

"The words aren't big or very many. Just three, in fact. And they're only one syllable apiece."

"That simple?"

"Yeah."

Steve figured he needed something more than three words to stack the deck in his favor. He draped his arm loosely across Nick's shoulders. "I've got an idea. Do you really want to make it up to me?"

"Not if it involves seminudity or screaming like a chicken in public."

"The only requirement is an extra pair of hands and a strong back."

Feeling only slight discomfort from the birth, Rosie sat in her hospital room chair waiting to go home. It had been two days since she'd unburdened herself to her mother. Flo Marchetti had made a convincing case for fighting for her man. Rosie smiled at the memory of her mother's story about confronting her father. She'd always thought love was like spontaneous combustion. It just happened, then there was "happy ever after." Her parents made it look easy. She'd never realized that there was risk involved.

She glanced covertly at Steve. He held the baby while they waited for the business office rep to come in and get the information for the birth certificate. After that, it was time to go. She had never understood the meaning of the word "bittersweet" more than she did at this moment.

She could hardly wait to get her little girl home.

At the same time, it was the beginning of the end for her and Steve. She figured he would wait a decent interval, sleeping on that silly air mattress in her living room. Then he would walk out of her life. Unless telling him she loved him could make the difference. She'd made up her mind to fight for him, but she was so afraid she wouldn't be enough to convince him to stay.

Tears sprang to her eyes and she blinked furiously. She wouldn't go to the pity place, *not* today, and definitely not in front of Steve. She'd had enough of his pity to last her a lifetime. If they were going to survive, it would be for love, or not at all.

A woman with a clipboard in hand appeared in the doorway. Auburn-haired, with granny glasses perched on the end of her nose, she smiled warmly at the tender sight of Steve with an infant in his arms. He looked as if he hadn't slept in days. Rosie sighed. No man with fatigue written all over his face should look that good, she thought.

"I'm Marilyn Knox." The woman cleared her throat. "Mr. and Mrs. Schafer, you've put this off long enough. It's time to pick a name for this little girl."

With her pen poised above the paper, she waited while Rosie looked at Steve. This was the moment of truth. Rosie knew he would keep silent, let her decide. She had, but wasn't sure what he would think.

Mrs. Knox looked from one to the other, then sat on the side of the bed with a big sigh. "Let's start with something easy, like the last name."

"Schafer," Steve said in a loud, clear, firm voice.

The tears Rosie had been battling were back again. In front of God and everyone, he was declaring legal and moral responsibility for her child. He was a good man. What would it take to convince him of that fact?

"There, that wasn't so hard," Mrs. Knox said. "Now, a first name would be good so we don't have to keep calling her Baby Girl Schafer."

Rosie took a deep breath. "Stephanie Nicole."

"Stephanie?" Steve's gaze snapped to hers so fast whiplash was a real possibility. "Nicole?"

Rosie nodded. "After two of the most important men in my life."

"Stephanie Nicole Schafer." Mrs. Knox stood and peeked at the infant in Steve's arms. "It's a lovely name for a beautiful little girl. Good luck, you two," she said.

When they were alone, Steve put the baby in Rosie's arms. "Nurse Ratchett said to pull the car around the front of the hospital and she would take you out in a wheelchair."

"You shouldn't call Liz that. She's a good nurse, protective of her patients. Just because Joey started that name—"

"She took good care of you and Stephanie. That's all I care about."

There he was, being sweet again. Rosie was grateful that he turned his back to pick up her suitcase. It kept him from seeing her expression. He also grabbed an armful of stuff. "You've only been here a couple of days. Where did all this come from?"

"Four uncles and doting grandparents who refuse to walk in the door empty-handed. My apartment is going to be filled to the rafters by the time she's a month old."

Steve gave her an odd look, then continued to organize everything. He managed to gather it all in one load and then left her room. Through her tears, Rosie stared at her baby.

"Stephanie Schafer, I hope you like your name. It will always remind us of your father."

Rosie was so preoccupied watching the baby, securely belted and harnessed in the car seat behind her, she didn't realize where they were until Steve shut off the car.

She looked around. "This is your condo."

"I know."

"I figured you knew. That was an invitation for an explanation. Why did you bring us here? I don't understand, Steve."

"Why don't we take the baby inside first?"

Rosie's mind whirled as Steve unhooked the car seat, gripped the handle, and lifted it out as if Stephanie were the most precious thing in the world. Why had he brought them here? Did she dare hope?

Steve lead her inside and she looked around. He'd had the place redecorated since the last time she'd been there. She wasn't clear on how she knew that. The last time she'd found him with a woman and she figured under those circumstances observation and humiliation were mutually exclusive. It surprised her that he chose a color scheme that was her favorite— hunter green and mauve. Should she read anything into that?

"Follow me, Ro."

She nodded and they went up a few stairs into the bedroom next to the master. It was unbelievable. Inside was a completely put together baby nursery including the furniture she'd picked out for a girl. There was a canopy crib, made of light blond wood. An armoire stood beside the matching combination dresser and changing table. The theme was a popular, whimsical cartoon character. Stuffed animals adorned every available space. But the coup de grace was the state-of-the-art baby swing in the corner.

She had pointed it out to him once when they'd meandered through the baby store at the mall. She'd thought he hadn't been paying attention. She'd been wrong. Everything she'd oohed and ahed and coveted was here. It was a dream nursery.

Stunned, she touched a trembling hand to her mouth.

"When did you do all this?"

"Wallpaper would be nice, but I didn't have time."

"I can't believe you did what you did. How?"

"Nick helped."

"He did?" Those darn tears always seemed to be right there, she thought, annoyed. She looked at him, shaking her head in wonder. "I love it. Can we try her in the swing?"

"Sure." He looked at the tiny infant, then sheepishly back to Rosie. "If you put her in."

She smiled at him. "Sure."

Carefully, she picked up her wide-awake daughter and placed her in the padded seat. She buckled her in and, for good measure, tucked receiving blankets around the infant. Then she studied the digital control. After selecting "one" for the slowest speed, the seat started to sway gently.

Rosie stood on one side of the swing and Steve on the other. When she knew all was fine with the swinging baby, her gaze strayed to the man who had always made her heart beat like a teenage girl with her first crush. Now was no exception, especially when she realized he'd been watching her. And there was a look in his eyes of hope and hunger.

She'd been an idiot not to know that he had something to say to her. But after everything, she was afraid to trust that there was a chance for them. Quickly, she glanced back to the baby and watched her eyes drift shut.

"She's sleeping like a baby." Rosie looked at Steve. "I have a feeling this contraption is going to be a godsend."

"We should put her to bed," he said, and it was more question than stated fact.

"I think so," she answered, unable to shake the feeling that there was another surprise.

"Good. I can't wait to show you this." Without waking her, he extricated the sleeping infant from seat belt, blankets, and swing, and carried her into the master bedroom.

In the corner next to the king-size bed was the sweetest bassinet she'd ever seen. It was circular and covered in white satin, with lace curtains that draped down.

"All right." Rosie lifted the infant and placed her in the bed. When she started to squirm, Steve rocked it until she was sleeping soundly again.

"I think she likes it here," he said. He turned on the nursery monitor and took the other half that would allow them to hear the baby from anywhere in the condo.

Rosie took his hand and with fingers intertwined, they walked into the hall, then down to the living room. She sat on the green-and-beige plaid sofa in front of the fireplace.

"What are we doing here?" she asked, looking up at him.

He cast a sweeping glance around the room. "It's bigger and we need more space."

"We?" Hope bloomed in her heart like flowers waiting for the first spring sunshine after a very long winter.

He sat beside her, so close that his thigh brushed hers. She loved the tender expression in his blue eyes.

"I want you to stay. You and Stephanie." He hesitated.

This was her chance. It was now or never. She had to fight for her man and tell him how she felt.

She let the words come out and he spoke at the same time. "I love you," they both said together.

"What did you say?" she asked.

"I love you. What did *you* say?"

"I love you."

"Really?"

She could only nod as he took her face in his hands and kissed her. The warmth of his lips was too sweet for words. Her pulse raced as he told her with his mouth and his hands what was in his heart.

Finally, Steve pulled back and let out a long, shuddering breath. "Nick was right. That wasn't so hard."

"My brother, the confirmed bachelor, convinced you to say that?" Rosie blinked, trying to focus after his toe-curling kiss.

"Yup."

"That would imply that you two have buried the hatchet?"

"Yup. He helped me move all your stuff over."

Rosie was so happy at this moment she was almost afraid to rock the boat. But she had to know. "Ma said she didn't hire you to investigate Wayne. Why did you do it on your own?''

He shrugged. ''I suspected he was a sleaze, but you seemed serious about him. I needed a reason to break you up.''

''All you had to do was tell me you love me.''

''Easier said than done. The best friend I'd ever had told me a long time ago that it's uncool to go out with your buddy's sister. Translation, at least my interpretation—guys who have no family aren't good enough for a Marchetti.''

Rosie put her arms around his neck and snuggled close, letting her love encompass him. ''The next time I see Nick, I think I'll use Nurse Ratchett's method of manhandling one meddling Marchetti man. He's—''

''It wasn't him. My own parents hadn't wanted me enough to stick around. Why would anyone else?''

''Because you're a good man.''

''Maybe. But what kind of father could I be? I never had one—''

''What's my dad? Chopped liver? You spent a lot of time with my family. Some of the Marchetti magic must have rubbed off.''

Doubtful, he shook his head. ''I don't know.''

''Let's put this to rest once and for all.'' She half turned to him with a fist on her hip. ''You had a choice in this family thing. You decided to stay. Good God, Steve, you moved us in here lock, stock, and baby furniture. That means you're willing to work at being a father. As far as I'm concerned, Stephanie couldn't ask for a better dad than you.''

He grinned. ''I believe you.''

''Good.'' She smiled back. ''Now that you're okay,

can we talk about all the tall blondes who came before me?''

"I'd rather not—''

"You have your issues, I've got mine. What was that all about? Why should I believe you love me when every woman you ever dated was my exact opposite?''

"That's why.''

"Huh?''

"I've always loved you, Ro. But I didn't think I could have you. And I didn't want a cheap imitation. No reminders of you. Hence, only tall blondes.''

"So your secretary poses no threat?'' she asked, feigning annoyance.

"You're not jealous of Sandy? Is that why you got so weird after that day in my office?''

"I didn't get weird. What a thing to say to the mother of your daughter.''

She put up weak, token resistance as he pulled her into his arms. This was a place she wanted to stay forever. In her fantasies, she had never been as happy as she was now.

"You're jealous,'' he said. "Takes one to know one. I've wanted to rip the heart out of every guy you've ever dated. I've wanted you for as long as I can remember.''

"You've always had me. The first time you let me tag along with you, I knew you walked on water.''

"So your mother was telling the truth about your crush.''

"Have you ever thought about that word? An odd way to describe strong feelings for another person. But accurate. For years, I was crushed by what I felt for you, thinking I wasn't enough—pretty enough, thin enough, tall enough—''

He silenced her with his mouth. After a long, slow, drugging kiss, he folded her in his arms and pressed her to his chest, holding her as if he never planned to let her go.

"I had a crush on you, too. I tried to fight it, but it turned into love. I will love you until the day I die.''

"For a man of few words, that was the most eloquent declaration I have ever heard.''

"Believe it.''

"I do.''

"It's nice to know good things come in threes.''

"Huh?''

"When Nick stopped by the other day, I was thinking that bad stuff always happens in triplicate. Now there's you, and Steph, and me. The Schafer family. Has a nice ring to it, don't you think?''

"Oh, yes.''

Rosie didn't know how or why she'd gotten so lucky. Did she deserve this much happiness? She would do her best to be worthy. If she could have seen the future, she never would have questioned her vows that day in the wedding chapel. She'd been reluctant to commit herself to "as long as you both live.'' Now she knew that only forever would be enough time to love her stand-in groom.

He'd always been her best man.

* * * * *

SOMETIMES THE SMALLEST PACKAGES CAN LEAD TO THE BIGGEST SURPRISES!

Bundles of Joy

February 1999
A VOW, A RING, A BABY SWING
by Teresa Southwick (SR #1349)

Pregnant and alone, Rosie Marchetti had just been stood up at the altar. So family friend Steve Schafer stepped up the aisle and married her. Now Rosie is trying to convince him that this family was meant to be....

May 1999
THE BABY ARRANGEMENT
by Moyra Tarling (SR #1368)

Jared McAndrew has been searching for his son, and when he discovers Faith Nelson with his child he demands she come home with him. Can Faith convince Jared that he has the wrong mother — but the right bride?

Enjoy these stories of love and family. And look for future BUNDLES OF JOY titles from Leanna Wilson and Suzanne McMinn coming in the fall of 1999.

BUNDLES OF JOY
only from

™ *Silhouette*®

Available wherever Silhouette books are sold.

Look us up on-line at: http://www.romance.net

SRBOJJ-J

If you enjoyed what you just read,
then we've got an offer you can't resist!

Take 2 bestselling love stories FREE!
Plus get a FREE surprise gift!

Clip this page and mail it to Silhouette Reader Service™

IN U.S.A.	IN CANADA
3010 Walden Ave.	P.O. Box 609
P.O. Box 1867	Fort Erie, Ontario
Buffalo, N.Y. 14240-1867	L2A 5X3

YES! Please send me 2 free Silhouette Romance® novels and my free surprise gift. Then send me 6 brand-new novels every month, which I will receive months before they're available in stores. In the U.S.A., bill me at the bargain price of $2.90 plus 25¢ delivery per book and applicable sales tax, if any*. In Canada, bill me at the bargain price of $3.25 plus 25¢ delivery per book and applicable taxes**. That's the complete price and a savings of over 10% off the cover prices—what a great deal! I understand that accepting the 2 free books and gift places me under no obligation ever to buy any books. I can always return a shipment and cancel at any time. Even if I never buy another book from Silhouette, the 2 free books and gift are mine to keep forever. So why not take us up on our invitation. You'll be glad you did!

215 SEN CNE7
315 SEN CNE9

Name	(PLEASE PRINT)	
Address	Apt.#	
City	State/Prov.	Zip/Postal Code

* Terms and prices subject to change without notice. Sales tax applicable in N.Y.
** Canadian residents will be charged applicable provincial taxes and GST.
  All orders subject to approval. Offer limited to one per household.
  ® are registered trademarks of Harlequin Enterprises Limited.

SROM99   ©1998 Harlequin Enterprises Limited

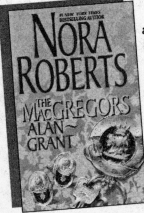

Based on the bestselling miniseries

FORTUNE'S *Children*™

A FORTUNE'S CHILDREN *Wedding:*
THE HOODWINKED BRIDE

by BARBARA BOSWELL

This March, the Fortune family discovers a twenty-six-year-old secret—beautiful Angelica Carroll *Fortune!* Kate Fortune hires Flynt Corrigan to protect the newest Fortune, and this jaded investigator soon finds this his most tantalizing—and tormenting—assignment to date....

Barbara Boswell's single title is just one of the captivating romances in Silhouette's exciting new miniseries, **Fortune's Children: The Brides,** featuring six special women who perpetuate a family legacy that is greater than mere riches!

Look for *The Honor Bound Groom,* by Jennifer Greene, when **Fortune's Children: The Brides** launches in Silhouette Desire in January 1999!

Available at your favorite retail outlet.

Silhouette®

Silhouette ROMANCE™

COMING NEXT MONTH

#1354 HUSBAND FROM 9 TO 5—Susan Meier
Loving the Boss

For days, Molly Doyle had thought she was Mrs. Jack Cavanaugh, and Jack played along—then she got her memory back, and realized she was only his *secretary*. So how could she convince her bachelor boss to make their pretend marriage real?

#1355 CALLAGHAN'S BRIDE—Diana Palmer
Virgin Brides Anniversary/Long Tall Texans

Callaghan Hart exasperated temporary ranch cook Tess Brady by refusing to admit that the attraction they shared was more than just passion. Could Tess make Callaghan see she was his truelove bride before her time on the Hart Ranch ran out?

#1356 A RING FOR CINDERELLA—Judy Christenberry
The Lucky Charm Sisters

The last thing Susan Greenwood expected when she went into her family's diner was a marriage proposal! But cowboy Zack Lowery was in desperate need of a fiancée to fulfill his grandfather's dying wish. Still, she was astonished at the power of pretense when *acting* in love started to feel a lot like *being* in love!

#1357 TEXAS BRIDE—Kate Thomas

Charming lawyer Josh Walker had always wanted a child. So when the woman who saved him from a car wreck went into labor, he was eager to care for her and her son. Yet lazy days—and nights—together soon had Josh wanting to make Dani *his*…forever!

#1358 SOLDIER AND THE SOCIETY GIRL—Vivian Leiber
He's My Hero

Refined protocol specialist Chessy Banks Bailey had thirty days to transform rough 'n' rugged, true-grit soldier Derek McKenna into a polished spokesman. Her mission seemed quite impossible…until lessons in etiquette suddenly turned into lessons in love….

#1359 SHERIFF TAKES A BRIDE—Gayle Kaye
Family Matters

Hallie Cates didn't pay much attention to the new sheriff in town—until Cam Osborne arrested her grandmother for moonshining! Hallie swore to prove her grandmother's innocence. But she was soon caught up in the strong, passionate arms of the law herself!